The Law of the
Four Just Men

HOUSE OF
STRATUS

Copyright by David William Shorey
as Executor of Mrs Margaret Penelope June Halcrow otherwise Penelope Wallace.

This edition published in 2001 by House of Stratus, an imprint of House of Stratus Ltd, Thirsk Industrial Park, York Road, Thirsk, North Yorkshire, YO7 3BX, UK.

www.houseofstratus.com

Typeset by House of Stratus, printed and bound by Short Run Press Limited.

A catalogue record for this book is available from the British Library and the Library of Congress.

ISBN 1-84232-693-7

We would like to thank the Edgar Wallace Society for all the support they have given House of Stratus. Enquiries on how to join the Edgar Wallace Society should be addressed to: The Edgar Wallace Society, c/o Penny Wyrd, 84 Ridgefield Road, Oxford, OX4 3DA. Email: info@edgarwallace.org Web: http://www.edgarwallace.org/

Edgar Wallace was born illegitimately in 1875 in Greenwich and adopted by George Freeman, a porter at Billingsgate fish market. At eleven, Wallace sold newspapers at Ludgate Circus and on leaving school took a job with a printer. He enlisted in the Royal West Kent Regiment, later transferring to the Medical Staff Corps, and was sent to South Africa. In 1898 he published a collection of poems called *The Mission that Failed*, left the army and became a correspondent for Reuters.

Wallace became the South African war correspondent for *The Daily Mail*. His articles were later published as *Unofficial Dispatches* and his outspokenness infuriated Kitchener, who banned him as a war correspondent until the First World War. He edited the *Rand Daily Mail*, but gambled disastrously on the South African Stock Market, returning to England to report on crimes and hanging trials. He became editor of *The Evening News*, then in 1905 founded the Tallis Press, publishing *Smithy*, a collection of soldier stories, and *Four Just Men*. At various times he worked on *The Standard*, *The Star*, *The Week-End Racing Supplement* and *The Story Journal*.

In 1917 he became a Special Constable at Lincoln's Inn and also a special interrogator for the War Office. His first marriage to Ivy Caldecott, daughter of a missionary, had ended in divorce and he married his much younger secretary, Violet King.

The Daily Mail sent Wallace to investigate atrocities in the Belgian Congo, a trip that provided material for his *Sanders of the River* books. In 1923 he became Chairman of the Press Club and in 1931 stood as a Liberal candidate at Blackpool. On being offered a scriptwriting contract at RKO, Wallace went to Hollywood. He died in 1932, on his way to work on the screenplay for *King Kong*.

BY THE SAME AUTHOR
ALL PUBLISHED BY HOUSE OF STRATUS

TO
JEFFREY BERNERD

CONTENTS

THE MAN WHO LIVED AT CLAPHAM

"The jury cannot accept the unsupported suggestion – unsupported even by the prisoner's testimony since he has not gone into the box – that Mr Noah Stedland is a blackmailer and that he obtained a large sum of money from the prisoner by this practice. That is a defence which is rather suggested by the cross-examination than by the production of evidence. The defence does not even tell us the nature of the threat which Stedland employed…'

The remainder of the summing up was creditable to the best traditions of the Bar, and the jury, without retiring, returned a verdict of "Guilty".

There was a rustle of movement in the court and a thin babble of whispered talk as the Judge fixed his pince-nez and began to write.

The man in the big oaken pen looked down at the pale drawn face of a girl turned to him from the well of the court and smiled encouragingly. For his part, he did not blanch and his grave eyes went back to the figure on the Bench – the puce-gowned, white-headed figure that was writing so industriously. What did a Judge write on these occasions, he wondered? Surely not a précis of the crime. He was impatient now to have done with it all; this airy court, these blurred rows of pink faces in the gloom of the public gallery, the indifferent counsel and particularly with the two men who had sat near the lawyer's pews watching him intently.

He wondered who they were, what interest they had in the proceedings. Perhaps they were foreign authors, securing first-hand impressions. They had the appearance of foreigners. One was very tall (he had seen him rise to his feet once), the other was slight and gave an impression of boyishness, though his hair was grey. They were both clean-shaven and both were dressed in black and balanced on their knees broad-brimmed hats of soft black felt.

A cough from the Judge brought his attention back to the Bench.

"Jeffrey Storr," said his lordship, "I entirely agree with the verdict of the jury. Your defence that Stedland robbed you of your savings and that you broke into his house for the purpose of taking the law into your own hands and securing the money and a document, the character of which you do not specify but which you allege proved his guilt, could not be considered seriously by any Court of Justice. Your story sounds as though you had read of that famous, or infamous, association called the Four Just Men, which existed some years ago, but which is now happily dispersed. Those men set themselves to punish where the law failed. It is a monstrous assumption that the law ever fails! You have committed a very serious offence, and the fact that you were at the moment of your arrest and capture in possession of a loaded revolver, serves very gravely to aggravate your crime. You will be kept in penal servitude for seven years."

Jeffrey Storr bowed and without so much as a glance at the girl in the court, turned and descended the steps leading to the cells.

The two foreign-looking men who had excited the prisoner's interest and resentment were the first to leave the court.

Once in the street the taller of the two stopped.

"I think we will wait for the girl," he said.

"Is she the wife?" asked the slight man.

"Married the week he made his unfortunate investment," replied the tall man, then, "it was a curious coincidence, that reference of the Judge's to the Four Just Men."

The other smiled.

"It was in that very court that you were sentenced to death, Manfred," he said, and the man called Manfred nodded.

"I wondered whether the old usher would remember me," he answered, "he has a reputation for never forgetting a face. Apparently the loss of my beard has worked a miracle, for I actually spoke to him. Here she is."

Fortunately the girl was alone. A beautiful face, thought Gonsalez, the younger of the two men. She held her chin high and there was no sign of tears. As she walked quickly toward Newgate Street they followed her. She crossed the road into Hatton Garden and then it was that Manfred spoke.

"Pardon me, Mrs Storr," he said, and she turned and stared at the foreign-looking man suspiciously.

"If you are a reporter – " she began.

"I'm not," smiled Manfred, "nor am I a friend of your husband's, though I thought of lying to you in that respect in order to find an excuse for talking to you."

His frankness procured her interest.

"I do not wish to talk about poor Jeffrey's terrible trouble," she said, "I just want to be alone."

Manfred nodded.

"I understand that," he said sympathetically, "but I wish to be a friend of your husband's and perhaps I can help him. The story he told in the box was true – you thought that too, Leon?"

Gonsalez nodded.

"Obviously true," he said, "I particularly noticed his eyelids. When a man lies he blinks at every repetition of the lie. Have you observed, my dear George, that men cannot tell lies when their hands are clenched and that when women lie they clasp their hands together?"

She looked at Gonsalez in bewilderment. She was in no mood for a lecture on the physiology of expression and even had she known that Leon Gonsalez was the author of three large books which ranked with the best that Lombroso or Mantegazza had given to the world, she would have been no more willing to listen.

"The truth is, Mrs Storr," said Manfred, interpreting her new distress, "we think that we can free your husband and prove his innocence. But we want as many facts about the case as we can get."

She hesitated only a moment.

3

"I have some furnished lodgings in Gray's Inn Road," she said, "perhaps you will be good enough to come with me.

"My lawyer does not think there is any use in appealing against the sentence," she went on as they fell in one on either side of her.

Manfred shook his head.

"The Appeal Court would uphold the sentence," he said quietly, "with the evidence you have there is no possibility of your husband being released."

She looked round at him in dismay and now he saw that she was very near to tears.

"I thought…you said…" she began a little shakily.

Manfred nodded.

"We know Stedland," he said, "and – "

"The curious thing about blackmailers, is that the occiput is hardly observable," interrupted Gonsalez thoughtfully. "I examined sixty-two heads in the Spanish prisons and in every case the occipital protuberance was little more than a bony ridge. Now in homicidal heads the occiput sticks out like a pigeon's egg."

"My friend is rather an authority upon the structure of the head," smiled Manfred. "Yes, we know Stedland. His operations have been reported to us from time to time. You remember the Wellingford case, Leon?"

Gonsalez nodded.

"Then you are detectives?" asked the girl.

Manfred laughed softly.

"No, we are not detectives – we are interested in crime. I think we have the best and most thorough record of the unconvicted criminal class of any in the world."

They walked on in silence for some time.

"Stedland is a bad man," nodded Gonsalez as though the conviction had suddenly dawned upon him. "Did you observe his ears? They are unusually long and the outer margins are pointed – the Darwinian tubercle, Manfred. And did you remark, my dear friend, that the root of the helix divides the concha into two distinct cavities and that the lobule was adherent? A truly criminal ear. The man has committed murder. It is impossible to possess such an ear and not to murder."

The flat to which she admitted them was small and wretchedly furnished. Glancing round the tiny dining-room, Manfred noted the essential appointments which accompany a "furnished" flat.

The girl, who had disappeared into her room to take off her coat, now returned, and sat by the table at which, at her invitation, they had seated themselves.

"I realise that I am being indiscreet," she said with the faintest of smiles; "but I feel that you really want to help me, and I have the curious sense that you can! The police have not been unkind or unfair to me and poor Jeff. On the contrary, they have been most helpful. I fancy that they suspected Mr Stedland of being a blackmailer, and they were hoping that we could supply some evidence. When that evidence failed, there was nothing for them to do but to press forward the charge. Now, what can I tell you?"

"The story which was not told in court," replied Manfred.

She was silent for a time.

"I will tell you," she said at last. "Only my husband's lawyer knows, and I have an idea that he was sceptical as to the truth of what I am now telling you. And if he is sceptical," she said in despair, "how can I expect to convince you?"

The eager eyes of Gonsalez were fixed on hers, and it was he who answered.

"We are already convinced, Mrs Storr," and Manfred nodded.

Again there was a pause. She was evidently reluctant to begin a narrative which, Manfred guessed, might not be creditable to her; and this proved to be the case.

"When I was a girl," she began simply, "I was at school in Sussex – a big girls' school; I think there were over two hundred pupils. I am not going to excuse anything I did," she went on quickly. "I fell in love with a boy – well, he was a butcher's boy! That sounds dreadful, doesn't it? But you understand I was a child, a very impressionable child – oh, it sounds horrible, I know; but I used to meet him in the garden leading out from the prep room after prayers; he climbed over the wall to those meetings, and we talked and talked, sometimes for an hour. There was no more in it than a boy and girl love affair, and I can't explain just why I committed such a folly."

"Mantegazza explains the matter very comfortably in his Study of Attraction," murmured Leon Gonsalez. "But forgive me, I interrupted you."

"As I say, it was a boy and girl friendship, a kind of hero worship on my part, for I thought he was wonderful. He must have been the nicest of butcher boys," she smiled again, "because he never offended me by so much as a word. The friendship burnt itself out in a month or two, and there the matter might have ended, but for the fact that I had been foolish enough to write letters. They were very ordinary, stupid love-letters, and perfectly innocent – or at least they seemed so to me at the time. Today, when I read them in the light of a greater knowledge they take my breath away."

"You have them, then?" said Manfred.

She shook her head.

"When I said 'them' I meant one, and I only have a copy of that, supplied by Mr Stedland. The one letter that was not destroyed fell into the hands of the boy's mother, who took it to the headmistress, and there was an awful row. She threatened to write to my parents who were in India, but on my solemn promise that the acquaintance should be dropped, the affair was allowed to blow over. How the letter came into Stedland's hands I do not know; in fact, I had never heard of the man until a week before my marriage with Jeff. Jeff had saved about two thousand pounds, and we were looking forward to our marriage day when this blow fell. A letter from a perfectly unknown man, asking me to see him at his office, gave me my first introduction to this villain. I had to take the letter with me, and I went in some curiosity, wondering why I had been sent for. I was not to wonder very long. He had a little office off Regent Street, and after he had very carefully taken away the letter he had sent me, he explained, fully and frankly, just what his summons had meant."

Manfred nodded.

"He wanted to sell you the letter," he said, "for how much?"

"For two thousand pounds. That was the diabolical wickedness of it," said the girl vehemently. "He knew almost to a penny how much Jeff had saved."

"Did he show you the letter?"

She shook her head.

"No, he showed me a photographic reproduction and as I read it and realised what construction might be put upon this perfectly innocent note, my blood went cold. There was nothing to do but to tell Jeff, because the man had threatened to send facsimiles to all our friends and to Jeffrey's uncle, who had made Jeffrey his sole heir. I had already told Jeffrey about what happened at school, thank heaven, and so I had no need to fear his suspicion. Jeffrey called on Mr Stedland, and I believe there was a stormy scene; but Stedland is a big, powerful man in spite of his age, and in the struggle which ensued poor Jeffrey got a little the worst of it. The upshot of the matter was, Jeffrey agreed to buy the letter for two thousand pounds, on condition that Stedland signed a receipt, written on a blank page of the letter itself. It meant the losing of his life savings; it meant the possible postponement of our wedding; but Jeffrey would not take any other course. Mr Stedland lives in a big house near Clapham Common – "

"184 Park View West," interrupted Manfred.

"You know?" she said in surprise. "Well, it was at this house Jeffrey had to call to complete the bargain. Mr Stedland lives alone except for a manservant, and opening the door himself, he conducted Jeffrey up to the first floor, where he had his study. My husband, realising the futility of argument, paid over the money, as he had been directed by Stedland, in American bills – "

"Which are more difficult to trace, of course," said Manfred.

"When he had paid him, Stedland produced the letter, wrote the receipt on the blank page, blotted it and placed it in an envelope, which he gave to my husband. When Jeffrey returned home and opened the envelope, he found it contained nothing more than a blank sheet of paper."

"He had rung the changes," said Manfred.

7

"That was the expression that Jeffrey used," said the girl. "Then it was that Jeffrey decided to commit this mad act. You have heard of the Four Just Men?"

"I have heard of them," replied Manfred gravely.

"My husband is a great believer in their methods, and a great admirer of them too," she said. "I think he read everything that has ever been written about them. One night, two days after we were married – I had insisted upon marrying him at once when I discovered the situation – he came to me.

" 'Grace,' he said, 'I am going to apply the methods of the Four to this devil Stedland.'

"He outlined his plans. He had apparently been watching the house, and knew that except for the servant the man slept in the house alone, and he had formed a plan for getting in. Poor dear, he was an indifferent burglar; but you heard today how he succeeded in reaching Stedland's room. I think he hoped to frighten the man with his revolver."

Manfred shook his head.

"Stedland graduated as a gun-fighter in South Africa," he said quietly. "He is the quickest man on the draw I know, and a deadly shot. Of course, he had your husband covered before he could as much as reach his pocket."

She nodded.

"That is the story," she said quietly. "If you can help Jeff, I shall pray for you all my life."

Manfred rose slowly.

"It was a mad attempt," he said. "In the first place Stedland would not keep a compromising document like that in his house, which he leaves for six hours a day. It might even have been destroyed, though that is unlikely. He would keep the letter for future use. Blackmailers are keen students of humanity, and he knows that money may still be made, from that letter of yours. But if it is in existence – "

"If it is in existence," she repeated – and now the reaction had come and her lips were trembling –

"I will place it in your hands within a week," said Manfred, and with this promise left her.

Mr Noah Stedland had left the Courts of Justice that afternoon with no particular sense of satisfaction save that he was leaving it by the public entrance. He was not a man who was easily scared, but he was sensitive to impressions; and it seemed to him that the Judge's carefully chosen words had implied, less in their substance than in their tone, a veiled rebuke to himself. Beyond registering this fact, his sensitiveness did not go. He was a man of comfortable fortune, and that fortune had been got together in scraps – sometimes the scraps were unusually large – by the exercise of qualities which were not handicapped by such imponderable factors as conscience or remorse. Life to this tall, broad-shouldered, grey-faced man was a game, and Jeffrey Storr, against whom he harboured no resentment, was a loser.

He could think dispassionately of Storr in his convict clothes, wearing out the years of agony in a convict prison, and at the mental picture could experience no other emotion than that of the successful gambler who can watch his rival's ruin with equanimity.

He let himself into his narrow-fronted house, closed and double-locked the door behind him, and went up the shabbily carpeted stairs to his study. The ghosts of the lives he had wrecked should have crowded the room; but Mr Stedland did not believe in ghosts. He rubbed his finger along a mahogany table and noted that it was dusty, and the ghost of a well-paid charlady took shape from that moment.

As he sprawled back in his chair, a big cigar between his gold-spotted teeth, he tried to analyse the queer sensation he had experienced in court. It was not the Judge, it was not the attitude of the defending counsel, it was not even the possibility that the world might censure him, which was responsible for his mental perturbation. It was certainly not the prisoner and his possible fate, or the white-faced wife. And yet there had been a something or a somebody which had set him glancing uneasily over his shoulder.

He sat smoking for half an hour, and then a bell clanged and he went down the stairs and opened the front door. The man who was waiting with an apologetic smile on his face, a jackal of his, was butler and tout and general errand-boy to the hard-faced man.

"Come in, Jope," he said, closing the door behind the visitor. "Go down to the cellar and get me a bottle of whisky."

"How was my evidence, guv'nor?" asked the sycophant, smirking expectantly.

"Rotten," growled Stedland. "What did you mean by saying you heard me call for help?"

"Well, guv'nor, I thought I'd make it a little worse for him," said Jope humbly.

"Help!" sneered Mr Stedland. "Do you think I'd call on a guy like you for help? A damned lot of use you would be in a rough house! Get that whisky!"

When the man came up with a bottle and a siphon, Mr Stedland was gazing moodily out of the window which looked upon a short, untidy garden terminating in a high wall. Behind that was a space on which a building had been in course of erection when the armistice put an end to Government work. It was designed as a small factory for the making of fuses, and was an eyesore to Mr Stedland, since he owned the ground on which it was built.

"Jope," he said, turning suddenly, "was there anybody in court we know?"

"No, Mr Stedland," said the man, pausing in surprise. "Not that I know, except Inspector – "

"Never mind about the Inspector," answered Mr Stedland impatiently. "I know all the splits who were there. Was there anybody else – anybody who has a grudge against us?"

"No, Mr Stedland. What does it matter if there was?" asked the valorous Jope. "I think we're a match for any of 'em."

"How long have we been in partnership?" asked Stedland unpleasantly, as he poured himself out a tot of whisky.

The man's face twisted in an ingratiating smile.

"Well, we've been together some time now, Mr Stedland," he said.

Stedland smacked his lips and looked out of the window again.

"Yes," he said after a while, "we've been together a long time now. In fact, you would almost have finished your sentence, if I had told the police what I knew about you seven years ago – "

The man winced, and changed the subject. He might have realised, had he thought, that the sentence of seven years had been commuted by Stedland to a sentence of life servitude, but Mr Jope was no thinker.

"Anything for the Bank today, sir?" he asked.

"Don't be a fool," said Stedland. "The Bank closed at three. Now, Jope," he turned on the other, "in future you sleep in the kitchen."

"In the kitchen, sir?" said the astonished servant and Stedland nodded.

"I'm taking no more risks of a night visitor," he said. "That fellow was on me before I knew where I was, and if I hadn't had a gun handy he would have beaten me. The kitchen is the only way you can break into this house from the outside, and I've got a feeling at the back of my mind that something might happen."

"But he's gone to gaol."

"I'm not talking about him," snarled Stedland. "Do you understand, take your bed to the kitchen."

"It's a bit draughty – " began Jope.

"Take your bed to the kitchen," roared Stedland, glaring at the man.

"Certainly, sir," said Jope with alacrity.

When his servant had gone, Stedland took off his coat and put on one of stained alpaca, unlocked the safe, and took out a book. It was a passbook from his bank, and its study was very gratifying. Mr Stedland dreamed dreams of a South American ranch and a life of ease and quiet. Twelve years' strenuous work in London had made him a comparatively rich man. He had worked cautiously and patiently and had pursued the business of blackmail in a businesslike manner. His cash balance was with one of the best known of the private bankers, Sir William Molbury & Co., Ltd. Molbury's Bank had a reputation in the City for the privacy and even mystery which enveloped the business of its clients – a circumstance which suited Mr Stedland

11

admirably. It was, too, one of those old-fashioned banks which maintain a huge reserve of money in its vaults; and this was also a recommendation to Mr Stedland, who might wish to gather in his fluid assets in the shortest possible space of time.

The evening and the night passed without any untoward incident, except as was revealed when Mr Jope brought his master's tea in the morning, and told, somewhat hoarsely, of a cold and unpleasant night.

"Get more bedclothes," said Stedland curtly.

He went off to his city office after breakfast, and left Mr Jope to superintend the operations of the charwoman and to impress upon her a number of facts, including the high rate at which she was paid, the glut of good charwomen on the market and the consequences which would overtake her if she left Mr Stedland's study undusted.

At eleven o'clock that morning came a respectable and somewhat elderly looking gentleman in a silk hat, and him Mr Jope interviewed on the door-mat.

"I've come from the Safe Deposit," said the visitor.

"What Safe Deposit?" asked the suspicious Mr Jope.

'The Fetter Lane Deposit," replied the other. "We want to know if you left your keys behind the last time you came?"

Jope shook his head.

"We haven't any Safe Deposit," he said with assurance, "and the governor's hardly likely to leave his keys behind."

"Then evidently I've come to the wrong house," smiled the gentleman. "This is Mr Smithson's?"

"No, it ain't," said the ungracious Jope, and shut the door in the caller's face.

The visitor walked down the steps into the street and joined another man who was standing at a corner.

"They know nothing of Safe Deposits, Manfred," he said.

"I hardly thought it would be at a Safe Deposit," said the taller of the two. "In fact, I was pretty certain that he would keep all his papers at the bank. You saw the man Jope, I suppose?"

"Yes," said Gonsalez dreamily. "An interesting face. The chin weak, but the ears quite normal. The frontal bones slope irregularly backward, and the head, so far as I can see, is distinctly oxycephalic."

"Poor Jope!" said Manfred without a smile. "And now, Leon, you and I will devote our attention to the weather. There is an anticyclone coming up from the Bay of Biscay, and its beneficent effects are already felt in Eastbourne. If it extends northwards to London in the next three days we shall have good news for Mrs Storr."

"I suppose," said Gonsalez, as they were travelling back to their rooms in Jermyn Street, "I suppose there is no possibility of rushing this fellow."

Manfred shook his head.

"I do not wish to die," he said, "and die I certainly should, for Noah Stedland is unpleasantly quick to shoot."

Manfred's prophecy was fulfilled two days later, when the influence of the anticyclone spread to London and a thin yellow mist descended on the city. It lifted in the afternoon, Manfred saw to his satisfaction, but gave no evidence of dispersing before nightfall.

Mr Stedland's office in Regent Street was small but comfortably furnished. On the glass door beneath his name was inscribed the magic word: "Financier," and it is true that Stedland was registered as a moneylender and found it a profitable business; for what Stedland the moneylender discovered, Stedland the blackmailer exploited, and it was not an unusual circumstance for Mr Stedland to lend at heavy interest money which was destined for his own pocket. In this way he could obtain a double grip upon his victim.

At half past two that afternoon his clerk announced a caller.

"Man or woman?"

"A man, sir," said the clerk. "I think he's from Molbury's Bank."

"Do you know him?" asked Stedland.

"No, sir, but he came yesterday when you were out, and asked if you'd received the Bank's balance sheet."

Mr Stedland took a cigar from a box on the table and lit it.

"Show him in," he said, anticipating nothing more exciting than a dishonoured cheque from one of his clients.

13

The man who came in was obviously in a state of agitation. He closed the door behind him and stood nervously fingering his hat.

"Sit down," said Stedland. "Have a cigar, Mr – "

"Curtis, sir," said the other huskily. "Thank you, sir, I don't smoke."

"Well, what do you want?" asked Stedland.

"I want a few minutes' conversation with you, sir, of a private character." He glanced apprehensively at the glass partition which separated Mr Stedland's office from the little den in which his clerks worked.

"Don't worry," said Stedland humorously. "I can guarantee that screen is sound-proof. What's your trouble?"

He scented a temporary embarrassment, and a bank clerk temporarily embarrassed might make a very useful tool for future use.

"I hardly know how to begin, Mr Stedland," said the man, seating himself on the edge of a chair, his face twitching nervously. "It's a terrible story, a terrible story."

Stedland had heard about these terrible stories before, and sometimes they meant no more than that the visitor was threatened with bailiffs and was anxious to keep the news from the ears of his employers, sometimes the confession was more serious – money lost in gambling, and a desperate eleventh-hour attempt to make good a financial deficiency.

"Go on," he said. "You won't shock *me!*"

The boast was a little premature, however.

"It's not about myself, but about my brother, John Curtis, who's been cashier for twenty years, sir," said the man nervously. "I hadn't the slightest idea that he was in difficulties, but he was gambling on the Stock Exchange, and only today he has told me the news. I am in terrible distress about him, sir. I fear suicide. He is a nervous wreck."

"What has he done?" asked Stedland impatiently.

"He has robbed the Bank, sir," said the man in a hushed voice. "It wouldn't matter if it had happened two years ago, but now, when things have been going so badly and we've had to stretch a point to make our balance sheet plausible, I shudder to think what the results will be."

"Of how much has he robbed the Bank?" asked Stedland quickly.

"A hundred and fifty thousand pounds," was the staggering reply, and Stedland jumped to his feet.

"A hundred and fifty thousand?" he said incredulously.

"Yes, sir. I was wondering whether you could speak for him; you are one of the most highly respected clients of the Bank!"

"Speak for him!" shouted Stedland, and then of a sudden he became cool. His quick brain went over the situation, reviewing every possibility. He looked up at the clock. It was a quarter to three.

"Does anybody in the Bank know?"

"Not yet, sir, but I feel it is my duty to the general manager to tell him the tragic story. After the Bank closes this afternoon I am asking him to see me privately and – "

"Are you going back to the Bank now?" asked Stedland.

"Yes, sir," said the man in surprise.

"Listen to me, my friend," Stedland's grey face was set and tense. He took a case from his pocket, opened it and extracted two notes. "Here are two notes for fifty," he said. "Take those and go home."

"But I've got to go to the Bank, sir. They will wonder – "

"Never mind what they wonder," said Stedland. "You'll have a very good explanation when the truth comes out. Will you do this?"

The man took up the money reluctantly.

"I don't quite know what you – "

"Never mind what I want to do," snapped Stedland. "That is to keep your mouth shut and go home. Do you understand plain English?"

"Yes, sir," said the shaking Curtis.

Five minutes later Mr Stedland passed through the glass doors of Molbury's Bank and walked straight to the counter. An air of calm pervaded the establishment and the cashier, who knew Stedland, came forward with a smile.

> *"Unconscious of their awful doom,*
> *The little victims play,"*

quoted Stedland to himself. It was a favourite quotation of his, and he had used it on many appropriate occasions.

He passed a slip of paper across the counter, and the cashier looked at it and raised his eyebrows.

"Why, this is almost your balance, Mr Stedland," he said.

Stedland nodded.

"Yes, I am going abroad in a hurry," he said. "I shall not be back for two years, but I am leaving just enough to keep the account running."

It was a boast of Molbury's that they never argued on such occasions as these.

"Then you will want your box?" said the cashier politely.

"If you please," said Mr Noah Stedland. If the Bank passed into the hands of the Receiver, he had no wish for prying strangers to be unlocking and examining the contents of the tin box he had deposited with the Bank, and to the contents of which he made additions from time to time.

Ten minutes later, with close on a hundred thousand pounds in his pockets, a tin box in one hand, the other resting on his hip pocket – for he took no chances – Mr Stedland went out again in the street and into the waiting taxicab. The fog was cleared, and the sun was shining at Clapham when he arrived.

He went straight up to his study, fastened the door and unlocked the little safe. Into this he pushed the small box and two thick bundles of notes, locking the safe door behind him. Then he rang for the faithful Jope, unfastening the door to admit him.

"Have we another camp bed in the house?" he asked.

"Yes, sir," said Jope.

"Well, bring it up here. I am going to sleep in my study tonight."

"Anything wrong, sir?"

"Don't ask jackass questions. Do as you're told!"

Tomorrow, he thought, he would seek out a safer repository for his treasures. He spent that evening in his study and lay down to rest, but not to sleep, with a revolver on his chair by the side of his camp bed. Mr Stedland was a cautious man. Despite his intention to dispense with sleep for one night, he was dozing when a sound in the street outside roused him.

It was a familiar sound – the clang of fire bells – and apparently fire engines were in the street, for he heard the whine of motors and the sound of voices. He sniffed; there was a strong smell of burning, and looking up he saw a flicker of light reflected on the ceiling. He sprang out of bed to discover the cause. It was immediately discernible, for the fuse factory was burning merrily, and he caught a glimpse of firemen at work and a momentary vision of a hose in action. Mr Stedland permitted himself to smile. That fire would be worth money to him, and there was no danger to himself.

And then he heard a sound in the hall below; a deep voice boomed an order, and he caught the chatter of Jope, and unlocked the door. The lights were burning in the hall and on the stairway. Looking over the banisters he saw the shivering Jope, with an overcoat over his pyjamas, expostulating with a helmeted fireman.

"I can't help it," the latter was saying, "I've got to get a hose through one of these houses, and it might as well be yours."

Mr Stedland had no desire to have a hose through his house, and thought he knew an argument which might pass the inconvenience on to his neighbour.

"Just come up here a moment," he said. "I want to speak to one of those firemen."

The fireman came clumping up the stairs in his heavy boots, a fine figure of a man in his glittering brass.

"Sorry," he said, "but I must get the hose – "

"Wait a moment, my friend," said Mr Stedland with a smile. "I think you will understand me after a while. There are plenty of houses in this road, and a tenner goes a long way, eh? Come in."

He walked back into his room and the fireman followed and stood watching as he unlocked the safe. Then:

"I didn't think it would be so easy," he said.

Stedland swung round.

"Put up your hands," said the fireman, "and don't make trouble, or you're going out, Noah. I'd just as soon kill you as talk to you."

Then Noah Stedland saw that beneath the shade of the helmet the man's face was covered with a black mask.

"Who – who are you?" he asked hoarsely.

"I'm one of the Four Just Men – greatly reviled and prematurely mourned. Death is my favourite panacea for all ills…"

At nine o'clock in the morning Mr Noah Stedland still sat biting his nails, a cold uneaten breakfast spread on a table before him.

To him came Mr Jope wailing tidings of disaster, interrupted by Chief Inspector Holloway and a hefty subordinate who followed the servant into the room.

"Coming for a little walk with me, Stedland?" asked the cheery inspector, and Stedland rose heavily.

"What's the charge?" he asked heavily.

"Blackmail," replied the officer. "We've got evidence enough to hang you – delivered by special messenger. You fixed that case against Storr too – naughty, naughty!"

As Mr Stedland put on his coat the inspector asked:

"Who gave you away?"

Mr Stedland made no reply. Manfred's last words before he vanished into the foggy street had been emphatic.

"If he wanted to kill you, the man called Curtis would have killed you this afternoon when we played on your cunning; we would have killed you as easily as we set fire to the factory. And if you talk to the police of the Four Just Men, we will kill you, even though you be in Pentonville with a regiment of soldiers round you."

And somehow Mr Stedland knew that his enemy spoke the truth. So he said nothing, neither there nor in the dock at the Old Bailey, and went to penal servitude without speaking.

THE MAN WITH THE CANINE TEETH

"Murder, my dear Manfred is the most accidental of crimes," said Leon Gonsalez, removing his big shell-rimmed glasses and looking across the breakfast-table with that whimsical earnestness which was ever a delight to the handsome genius who directed the operations of the Four Just Men.

"Poiccart used to say that murder was a tangible expression of hysteria," he smiled, "but why this grisly breakfast-table topic?"

Gonsalez put on his glasses again and returned, apparently, to his study of the morning newspaper. He did not wilfully ignore the question, but his mind, as George Manfred knew, was so completely occupied by his reflections that he neither heard the query nor, for the matter of that, was he reading the newspaper. Presently he spoke again.

"Eighty per cent of the men who are charged with murder are making their appearance in a criminal court for the first time," he said; "therefore, murderers as a class are not criminals – I speak, of course, for the Anglo-Saxon murderer. Latin and Teutonic criminal classes supply sixty per cent of the murderers in France, Italy and the Germanic States. They are fascinating people, George, fascinating!"

His face lighted up with enthusiasm, and George Manfred surveyed him with amusement.

"I have never been able to take so detached a view of those gentlemen," he said. "To me they are completely horrible – for is not murder the apotheosis of injustice?"

"I suppose so," said Gonsalez vacantly.

"What started this line of thought?" asked Manfred, rolling his serviette.

"I met a true murderer type last night," answered the other calmly. "He asked me for a match and smiled when I gave it to him. A perfect set of teeth, my dear George, perfect – except – "

"Except?"

"The canine teeth were unusually large and long, the eyes deep set and amazingly level, the face anamorphic – which latter fact is not necessarily criminal."

"Sounds rather an ogre to me," said Manfred.

"On the contrary," Gonsalez hastened to correct the impression, "he was quite good-looking. None but a student would have noticed the irregularity of the face. Oh no, he was most presentable."

He explained the circumstances of the meeting. He had been to a recent concert the night before – not that he loved music, but because he wished to study the effect of music upon certain types of people. He had returned with hieroglyphics scribbled all over his programme., and had sat up half the night elaborating his notes.

"He is the son of Professor Tableman. He is not on good terms with his father, who apparently disapproves of his choice of fiancée, and he loathes his cousin," added Gonsalez simply.

Manfred laughed aloud.

"You amusing person! And did he tell you all this of his own free will, or did you hypnotise him and extract the information? You haven't asked me what I did last night."

Gonsalez was lighting a cigarette slowly and thoughtfully.

"He is nearly two metres – to be exact, six feet two inches – in height, powerfully built, with shoulders like that!" He held the cigarette in one hand and the burning match in the other to indicate the breadth of the young man. 'He has big, strong hands and plays football for the United Hospitals. I beg your pardon, Manfred; where *were* you last night?"

"At Scotland Yard," said Manfred; but if he expected to produce a sensation he was to be disappointed. Probably knowing his Leon, he anticipated no such result.

"An interesting building," said Gonsalez. "The architect should have turned the western façade southward – though its furtive entrances are in keeping with its character. You had no difficulty in making friends?"

"None. My work in connection with the Spanish Criminal Code and my monograph on Dactyology secured me admission to the chief."

Manfred was known in London as "Senor Fuentes," an eminent writer on criminology, and in their rôles of Spanish scientists both men bore the most compelling of credentials from the Spanish Minister of Justice. Manfred had made his home in Spain for many years. Gonsalez was a native of that country, and the third of the famous four – there had not been a fourth for twenty years – Poiccart, the stout and gentle, seldom left his big garden in Cordova.

To him Leon Gonsalez referred when he spoke.

"You must write and tell our dear friend Poiccart," he said. "He will be interested. I had a letter from him this morning. Two new litters of little pigs have come to bless his establishment, and his orange trees are in blossom."

He chuckled to himself, and then suddenly became serious.

"They took you to their bosom, these policemen?"

Manfred nodded.

"They were very kind and charming. We are lunching with one of the Assistant Commissioners, Mr Reginald Fare, tomorrow. British police methods have improved tremendously since we were in London before, Leon. The fingerprint department is a model of efficiency, and their new men are remarkably clever."

"They will hang us yet," said the cheerful Leon.

"I think not!" replied his companion.

The lunch at the Ritz-Carlton was, for Gonsalez especially, a most pleasant function. Mr Fare, the middle-aged Commissioner, was, in addition to being a charming gentleman, a very able scientist. The views and observations of Marro, Lombroso, Fere, Mantegazza and Ellis flew from one side of the table to the other.

"To the habitual criminal the world is an immense prison, alternating with an immense jag," said Fare. "That isn't my description but one a hundred years old. The habitual criminal is an easy man to deal with. It is when you come to the non-criminal classes, the murderers, the accidental embezzlers – "

"Exactly!" said Gonsalez. "Now my contention is – "

He was not to express his view, for a footman had brought an envelope to the Commissioner, and he interrupted Gonsalez with an apology to open and read its contents.

"H'm!" he said. "That is a curious coincidence…"

He looked at Manfred thoughtfully.

"You were saying the other night that you would like to watch Scotland Yard at work close at hand, and I promised you that I would give you the first opportunity which presented – your chance has come!"

He had beckoned the waiter and paid his bill before he spoke again.

"I shall not disdain to draw upon your ripe experience," he said, "for it is possible we may need all the assistance we can get in this case."

"What is it?" asked Manfred, as the Commissioner's car threaded the traffic at Hyde Park Corner.

"A man has been found dead in extraordinary circumstances," said the Commmissioner. "He holds rather a prominent position in the scientific world – a Professor Tableman – you probably know the name."

"Tableman?" said Gonsalez, his eyes opening wide. "Well, that is extraordinary! You were talking of coincidences, Mr Fare. Now I will tell you of another."

He related his meeting with the son of the Professor on the previous night.

"Personally," Gonsalez went on, "I look upon all coincidences as part of normal intercourse. It is a coincidence that, if you receive a bill requiring payment, you receive two or more during the day, and that if you receive a cheque by the first post, be sure you will receive a cheque by your second or third post. Some day I shall devote my mind to the investigation of that phenomenon."

"Professor Tableman lives in Chelsea. Some years ago he purchased his house from an artist, and had the roomy studio converted into a laboratory. He was a lecturer in physics and chemistry at the Bloomsbury University," explained Fare, though he need not have done so, for Manfred recalled the name; "and he was also a man of considerable means."

"I knew the Professor and dined with him about a month ago," said Fare. "He had had some trouble with his son. Tableman was an arbitrary, unyielding old man, one of those types of Christians who worship the historical figures of the Old Testament but never seem to get to the second book."

They arrived at the house, a handsome modern structure in one of the streets abutting upon King's Road, and apparently the news of the tragedy had not leaked out, for the usual crowd of morbid loungers had not gathered. A detective was waiting for them, and conducted the Commissioner along a covered passageway running by the side of the house, and up a flight of steps directly into the studio. There was nothing unusual about the room save that it was very light, for one of the walls was a huge window and the sloping roof was also of glass. Broad benches ran the length of two walls, and a big table occupied the centre of the room, all these being covered with scientific apparatus, whilst two long shelves above the benches were filled with bottles and jars, apparently containing chemicals.

A sad-faced, good-looking young man rose from a chair as they entered.

"I am John Munsey," he said, "the Professor's nephew. You remember me, Mr Fare? I used to assist my uncle in his experiments."

Fare nodded. His eyes were occupied with the figure that lay upon the ground, between table and bench.

"I have not moved the Professor," said the young man in a low voice. "The detectives who came moved him slightly to assist the doctor in making his examination, but he has been left practically where he fell."

The body was that of an old man, tall and spare, and on the grey face was an unmistakable look of agony and terror.

"It looked like a case of strangling," said Fare. "Has any rope or cord been found?"

"No, sir," replied the young man. "That was the view which the detectives reached, and we made a very thorough search of the laboratory."

Gonsalez was kneeling by the body, looking with dispassionate interest at the lean neck. About the throat was a band of blue about four inches deep, and he thought at first that it was a material bandage of some diaphanous stuff, but on close inspection he saw that it was merely the discoloration of the skin. Then his keen eye rose to the table, near where the Professor fell.

"What is that?" he asked. He pointed to a small green bottle by the side of which was an empty glass.

"It is a bottle of crême de menthe," said the youth; "my uncle took a glass usually before retiring."

"May I?" asked Leon, and Fare nodded.

Gonsalez picked up the glass and smelt it, then held it to the light.

"This glass was not used for liqueur last night, so he was killed before he drank," the Commissioner said. "I'd like to hear the whole story from you, Mr Munsey. You sleep on the premises, I presume?"

After giving a few instructions to the detectives, the Commissioner followed the young man into a room which was evidently the late Professor's library.

"I have been my uncle's assistant and secretary for three years," he said, "and we have always been on the most affectionate terms. It was my uncle's practice to spend the morning in his library, the whole of the afternoon either in his laboratory or at his office at the University, and he invariably spent the hours between dinner and bedtime working at his experiments."

"Did he dine at home?" asked Fare.

"Invariably," replied Mr Munsey, "unless he had an evening lecture or there was a meeting of one of the societies with which he was connected, and in that case he dined at the Royal Society's Club in St James's Street.

"My uncle, as you probably know, Mr Fare, has had a serious disagreement with his son, Stephen Tableman, and my cousin and very good friend. I have done my best to reconcile them, and when, twelve months ago, my uncle sent for me in this very room and told me that he had altered his will and left the whole of his property to me and had cut his son entirely from his inheritance, I was greatly distressed. I went immediately to Stephen and begged him to lose no time in reconciling himself with the old man. Stephen just laughed and said he didn't care about the Professor's money, and that, sooner than give up Miss Faber – it was about his engagement that the quarrel occurred – he would cheerfully live on the small sum of money which his mother left him. I came back and saw the Professor and begged him to restore Stephen to his will. I admit," he half smiled, "that I expected and would appreciate a small legacy. I am following the same scientific course as the Professor followed in his early days, and I have ambitions to carry on his work. But the Professor would have none of my suggestion. He raved and stormed at me, and I thought it would be discreet to drop the subject, which I did. Nevertheless, I lost no opportunity of putting in a word for Stephen, and last week, when the Professor was in an unusually amiable frame of mind, I raised the whole question again and he agreed to see Stephen. They met in the laboratory; I was not present, but I believe that there was a terrible row. When I came in, Stephen had gone, and Mr Tableman was livid with rage. Apparently, he had again insisted upon Stephen giving up his fiancée, and Stephen had refused point-blank."

"How did Stephen arrive at the laboratory?" asked Gonsalez. "May I ask that question, Mr Fare?"

The Commissioner nodded.

"He entered by the side passage. Very few people who come to the house on purely scientific business enter the house."

"Then access to the laboratory is possible at all hours?"

"Until the very last thing at night, when the gate is locked," said the young man. "You see, uncle used to take a little constitutional before going to bed, and he preferred using that entrance."

"Was the gate locked last night?"

John Munsey shook his head.

"No," he said quietly. "That was one of the first things I investigated. The gate was unfastened and ajar. It is not so much of a gate as an iron grille, as you probably observed."

"Go on," nodded Mr Fare.

"Well, the Professor gradually cooled down, and for two or three days he was very thoughtful, and I thought a little sad. On Monday – what is today? Thursday? – yes, it was on Monday, he said to me: 'John, let's have a little talk about Steve. Do you think I have treated him very badly?' 'I think you were rather unreasonable, Uncle,' I said. 'Perhaps I was,' he replied. 'She must be a very fine girl for Stephen to risk poverty for her sake.' That was the opportunity I had been praying for, and I think I urged Stephen's case with an eloquence which he would have commended. The upshot of it was that the old man weakened and sent a wire to Stephen, asking him to see him last night. It must have been a struggle for the Professor to have got over his objection to Miss Faber; he was a fanatic on the question of heredity – "

"Heredity?" interrupted Manfred quickly. "What was wrong with Miss Faber?"

"I don't know," shrugged the other, "but the Professor had heard rumours that her father had died in an inebriates' home. I believe those rumours were baseless."

"What happened last night?" asked Fare.

"I understand that Stephen came," said Munsey. "I kept carefully out of the way; in fact, I spent my time in my room, writing off some arrears of correspondence. I came downstairs about half past eleven, but the Professor had not returned. Looking from this window you can see the wall of the laboratory, and as the lights were still on, I thought the Professor's conversation had been protracted, and, hoping that the best results might come from this interview, I went to bed. It was earlier than I go as a rule, but it was quite usual for me to go to bed even without saying good night to the Professor.

"I was awakened at eight in the morning by the housekeeper, who told me that the Professor was not in his room. Here again, this was not an unusual circumstance. Sometimes the Professor would work very late in the laboratory and then throw himself into an armchair and go off to sleep. It was a habit of which I had remonstrated as plainly as I dared; but he was not a man who bore criticism with equanimity.

"I got into my dressing-gown and my slippers, and went along to the laboratory, which is reached, as you know, by the way we came here. It was than that I discovered him on the floor, and he was quite dead."

"Was the door of the laboratory open?" asked Gonsalez.

"It was ajar."

"And the gate also was ajar?"

Munsey nodded.

"You heard no sound of quarrelling?"

"None."

There was a knock, and Munsey walked to the door.

"It is Stephen," he said, and a second later Stephen Tableman, escorted by two detectives, came into the room. His big face was pale, and when he greeted his cousin with a little smile, Manfred saw the extraordinary canines, big and cruel looking. The other teeth were of normal size, but these pointed fangs were notably abnormal.

Stephen Tableman was a young giant, and, observing those great hands of his, Manfred bit his lip thoughtfully.

"You have heard the sad news, Mr Tableman?"

"Yes, sir," said Stephen in a shaking voice. "Can I see my father?"

"In a little time," said Fare, and his voice was hard. "I want you to tell me when you saw your father last."

"I saw him alive last night," said Stephen Tableman quickly. "I came by appointment to the laboratory, and we had a long talk."

"How long were you there with him?"

"About two hours, as near as I can guess."

"Was the conversation of a friendly character?"

"Very," said Stephen emphatically. "For the first time since over a year ago" – he hesitated – "we discussed a certain subject rationally."

"The subject being your fiancée, Miss Faber?"

Stephen looked at the interrogator steadily.

"That was the subject, Mr Fare," he replied quietly.

"Did you discuss any other matters?"

Stephen hesitated.

"We discussed money," he said. "My father cut off his allowance, and I have been rather short; in fact, I have been overdrawn at my bank, and he promised to make that right, and also spoke about – the future."

"About his will?"

"Yes, sir, he spoke about altering his will." He looked across at Munsey, and again he smiled. "My cousin has been a most persistent advocate, and I can't thank him half enough for his loyalty to me in those dark times," he said.

"When you left the laboratory, did you go out by the side entrance?"

Stephen nodded.

"And did you close the door behind you?"

"My father closed the door," he said. "I distinctly remember hearing the click of the lock as I was going up the alley."

"Can the door be opened from outside?"

"Yes," said Stephen, "there is a lock which has only one key, and that is in my father's possession – I think I am right, John?"

John Munsey nodded.

"So that, if he closed the door behind you, it could only be opened again by somebody in the laboratory – himself, for example?"

Stephen looked puzzled.

"I don't quite understand the meaning of this enquiry," he said. "The detective told me that my father had been found dead. What was the cause?"

"I think he was strangled," said Fare quietly, and the young man took a step back.

"Strangled!" he whispered. "But he hadn't an enemy in the world."

"That we shall discover." Fare's voice was dry and businesslike. "You can go now, Mr Tableman."

After a moment's hesitation the big fellow swung across the room through a door in the direction of the laboratory. He came back after an absence of a quarter of an hour, and his face was deathly white.

"Horrible, horrible!" he muttered. "My poor father!"

"You are on the way to being a doctor, Mr Tableman? I believe you are at the Middlesex Hospital," said Fare. "Do you agree with me that your father was strangled?"

The other nodded.

"It looks that way," he said, speaking with difficulty. "I couldn't conduct an examination as if he had been – somebody else, but it looks that way."

The two men walked back to their lodgings. Manfred thought best when his muscles were most active. Their walk was in silence, each being busy with his own thoughts.

"You observed the canines?" asked Leon with quiet triumph after a while.

"I observed too his obvious distress," said Manfred, and Leon chuckled.

"It is evident that you have not read friend Mantegazza's admirable monograph on the 'Physiology of Pain,'" he said smugly – Leon was delightfully smug at times – "nor examined his most admirable tables on the 'Synonyms of Expression,' or otherwise you would be aware that the expression of sorrow is indistinguishable from the expression of remorse."

Manfred looked down at his friend with that quiet smile of his.

"Anybody who did not know you, Leon, would say that you were convinced that Professor Tableman was strangled by his son."

"After a heated quarrel," said Gonsalez complacently.

"When young Tableman had gone, you inspected the laboratory. Did you discover anything?"

"Nothing more than I expected to find," said Gonsalez. "There were the usual air apparatus, the inevitable liquid-air still, the ever-to-be-expected electric crucibles. The inspection was superfluous, I admit, for I knew exactly how the murder was committed – for murder it was – the moment I came into the laboratory and saw the thermos flask and the pad of cotton wool."

Suddenly he frowned and stopped dead.

"*Santa Miranda!*" he ejaculated. Gonsalez always swore by this non-existent saint. "I had forgotten!"

He looked up and down the street.

"There is a place from whence we can telephone," he said. "Will you come with me, or shall I leave you here?"

"I am consumed with curiosity," said Manfred.

They went into the shop and Gonsalez gave a number. Manfred did not ask him how he knew it, because he too had read the number which was written on the telephone disc that stood on the late Professor's table.

"Is that you, Mr Munsey?" asked Gonsalez. "It is I. You remember I have just come from you?… Yes, I thought you would recognise my voice. I want to ask you where are the Professor's spectacles."

There was a moment's silence.

"The Professor's spectacles?" said Munsey's voice. "Why, they're with him, aren't they?"

"They were not on the body or near it," said Gonsalez. "Will you see if they are in his room? I'll hold the line."

He waited, humming a little aria from *El Perro Chico*, a light opera which had its day in Madrid fifteen years before; and presently he directed his attention again to the instrument.

"In his bedroom, were they? Thank you very much."

He hung up the receiver. He did not explain the conversation to Manfred, nor did Manfred expect him to, for Leon Gonsalez dearly loved a mystery. All he permitted himself to say was:

"Canine teeth!"

And this seemed to amuse him very much.

When Gonsalez came to breakfast the next morning, the waiter informed him that Manfred had gone out early. George came in about ten minutes after the other had commenced breakfast, and Leon Gonsalez looked up.

"You puzzle me when your face is so mask-like, George," he said. "I don't know whether you're particularly amused or particularly depressed."

"A little of the one and a little of the other," said Manfred, sitting down to breakfast. "I have been to Fleet Street to examine the files of the sporting press."

"The sporting press?" repeated Gonsalez, staring at him, and Manfred nodded.

"Incidentally, I met Fare. No trace of poison has been found in the body, and no other sign of violence. They are arresting Stephen Tableman today."

"I was afraid of that," said Gonsalez gravely. "But why the sporting press, George?"

Manfred did not answer the question, but went on:

"Fare is quite certain that the murder was committed by Stephen Tableman. His theory is that there was a quarrel and that the young man lost his temper and choked his father. Apparently, the examination of the body proved that extraordinary violence must have been used. Every blood-vessel in the neck is congested. Fare also told me that at first the doctor suspected poison, but there is no sign of any drug to be discovered, and the doctors say that the drug that would cause that death with such symptoms is unknown. It makes it worse for Stephen Tableman because for the past few months he has been concentrating his studies upon obscure poisons."

Gonsalez stretched back in his chair, his hands in his pockets.

"Well, whether he committed that murder or not," he said after a while, "he is certain to commit murder sooner or later. I remember once a doctor in Barcelona who had such teeth. He was a devout Christian, a popular man, a bachelor, and had plenty of money, and there seemed no reason in the world why he should murder anybody, and yet he did. He murdered another doctor who threatened to expose some error he had made in an operation. I tell you, George, with teeth like that – " He paused and frowned thoughtfully. "My dear

George," he said, "I am going to ask Fare if he will allow me the privilege of spending a few hours alone in Professor Tableman's laboratory."

"Why on earth – " began Manfred, and checked himself. "Why, of course, you have a reason, Leon. As a rule I find no difficulty in solving such mysteries as these. But in this case I am puzzled, though I have confidence that you have already unravelled what mystery there is. There are certain features about the business which are particularly baffling. Why should the old man be wearing thick gloves – "

Gonsalez sprang to his feet, his eyes blazing.

"What a fool! What a fool!" he almost shouted. "I didn't see those. Are you sure, George?" he asked eagerly. "He had thick gloves? Are you certain?"

Manfred nodded, smiling his surprise at the other's perturbation.

"That's it!" Gonsalez snapped his fingers. "I knew there was some error in my calculations! Thick woollen gloves, weren't they?" He became suddenly thoughtful. "Now, I wonder how the devil he induced the old man to put 'em on?" he said half to himself.

The request to Mr Fare was granted, and the two men went together to the laboratory. John Munsey was waiting for them.

"I discovered those spectacles by my uncle's bedside," he said as soon as he saw them.

"Oh, the spectacles?" said Leon absently. "May I see them?" He took them in his hand. "Your uncle was very short-sighted. How did they come to leave his possession, I wonder?"

"I think he went up to his bedroom to change; he usually did after dinner," explained Mr Munsey. "And he must have left them there. He usually kept an emergency pair in the laboratory, but for some reason or other he doesn't seem to have put them on. Do you wish to be alone in the laboratory?" he asked.

"I would rather," said Leon. "Perhaps you would entertain my friend whilst I look round?"

Left alone, he locked the door that communicated between the laboratory and the house, and his first search was for the spectacles that the old man usually wore when he was working.

Characteristically enough, he went straight to the place where they were – a big galvanised ash-pan by the side of the steps leading up to the laboratory. He found them in fragments, the horn rims broken in two places, and he collected what he could and returned to the laboratory, and, laying them on the bench, he took up the telephone.

The laboratory had a direct connection with the exchange, and after five minutes waiting, Gonsalez found himself in communication with Stephen Tableman.

"Yes, sir," was the surprised reply. "My father wore his glasses throughout the interview."

"Thank you, that is all," said Gonsalez and hung up the 'phone.

Then he went to one of the apparatus in a corner of the laboratory and worked steadily for an hour and a half. At the end of that time he went to the telephone again. Another half hour passed, and then he pulled from his pocket a pair of thick woollen gloves, and unlocking the door leading to the house, called Manfred.

"Ask Mr Munsey to come," he said.

"Your friend is interested in science," said Mr Munsey as they accompanied Manfred along the passage.

"I think he is one of the cleverest in his own particular line," said Manfred.

He came into the laboratory ahead of Munsey, and to his surprise, Gonsalez was standing near the table, holding in his hand a small liqueur glass filled with an almost colourless liquid. Almost colourless, but there was a blue tinge to it, and to Manfred's amazement a faint mist was rising from its surface.

Manfred stared at him, and then he saw that the hands of Leon Gonsalez were enclosed in thick woollen gloves.

"Have you finished?" smiled Mr Munsey as he came from behind Manfred; and then he saw Leon and smiled no more. His face went drawn and haggard, his eyes narrowed, and Manfred heard his laboured breathing.

"Have a drink, my friend?" said Leon pleasantly. "A beautiful drink. You'd mistake it for crême de menthe or any old liqueur – especially if you were a short-sighted, absent-minded old man and somebody had purloined your spectacles."

"What do you mean?" asked Munsey hoarsely. "I – I don't understand you."

"I promise you that this drink is innocuous, that it contains no poison whatsoever, that it is as pure as the air you breathe," Gonsalez went on.

"Damn you!" yelled Munsey, but before he could leap at his tormentor, Manfred had caught him and slung him to the ground.

"I have telephoned for the excellent Mr Fare, and he will be here soon, and also Mr Stephen Tableman. Ah, here they are."

There was a tap at the door.

"Will you open, please, my dear George? I do not think our young friend will move. If he does, I will throw the contents of this glass in his face."

Fare came in, followed by Stephen, and with them an officer from Scotland Yard.

"There is your prisoner, Mr Fare," said Gonsalez. "And here is the means by which Mr John Munsey encompassed the death of his uncle – decided thereto, I guess, by the fact that his uncle had been reconciled with Stephen Tableman, and that the will which he had so carefully manoeuvred was to be altered in Stephen Tableman's favour."

"That's a lie!" gasped John Munsey. "I worked for you – you know I did, Stephen. I did my best for you – "

"All part of the general scheme of deception – again I am guessing," said Gonsalez. "If I am wrong, drink this. It is the liquid your uncle drank on the night of his death."

"What is it?" demanded Fare quickly.

"Ask him," smiled Gonsalez, nodding to the man.

John Munsey turned on his heels and walked to the door, and the police officer who had accompanied Fare followed him.

"And now I will tell you what it is," said Gonsalez. "It is liquid air!"

"Liquid air!" said the Commissioner. "Why, what do you mean? How can a man be poisoned with liquid air?"

"Professor Tableman was not poisoned. Liquid air is a fluid obtained by reducing the temperature of air to two hundred and seventy degrees below zero. Scientists use the liquid for experiments, and it is usually kept in a thermos flask, the mouth of which is stopped with cotton wool, because, as you know, there would be danger of a blow up if the air was confined."

"Good God!" gasped Tableman in horror. "Then that blue mark about my father's throat – "

"He was frozen to death. At least his throat was frozen solid the second that liquid was taken. Your father was in the habit of drinking a liqueur before he went to bed, and there is no doubt that, after you had left, Munsey gave the Professor a glassful of liquid air and by some means induced him to put on gloves."

"Why did he do that? Oh, of course, the cold," said Manfred.

Gonsalez nodded.

"Without gloves he would have detected immediately the stuff he was handling. What artifice Munsey used we may never know. It is certain he himself must have been wearing gloves at the time. After your father's death he then began to prepare evidence to incriminate somebody else. The Professor had probably put away his glasses preparatory to going to bed, and the murderer, like myself, overlooked the fact that the body was still wearing gloves."

"My own theory," said Gonsalez later, "is that Munsey has been working for years to oust his cousin from his father's affections. He probably invented the story of the dipsomaniac father of Miss Faber."

Young Tableman had come to their lodgings, and now Gonsalez had a shock. Something he said had surprised a laugh from Stephen, and Gonsalez stared at him.

"Your – your teeth!" he stammered.

Stephen flushed.

"My teeth?" he repeated, puzzled.

"You had two enormous canines when I saw you last," said Gonsalez. "You remember, Manfred?" he said, and he was really agitated. "I told you – "

He was interrupted by a burst of laughter from the young student.

"Oh, they were false," he said awkwardly. "They were knocked out at a rugger match, and Benson, who's a fellow in our dental department and is an awfully good chap, though a pretty poor dentist, undertook to make me two to fill the deficiency. They looked terrible, didn't they? I don't wonder your noticing them. I got two new ones put in by another dentist."

"It happened on the thirteenth of September last year. I read about it in the sporting press," said Manfred, and Gonsalez fixed him with a reproachful glance.

"You see, my dear Leon – " Manfred laid his hand on the other's shoulder – "I knew they were false, just as you knew they were canines."

When they were alone, Manfred said:

"Talking about canines – "

"Let us talk about something else," snapped Leon.

THE MAN WHO HATED EARTHWORMS

"The death has occurred at Staines of Mr Falmouth, late Superintendent of the Criminal Investigation Department. Mr Falmouth will be best remembered as the Officer who arrested George Manfred, the leader of the Four Just Men gang. The sensational escape of this notorious man is perhaps the most remarkable chapter in criminal history. The 'Four Just Men' was an organisation which set itself to right acts of injustice which the law left unpunished. It is believed that the members were exceedingly rich men who devoted their lives and fortunes to this quixotic but wholly unlawful purpose. The gang has not been heard of for many years."

Manfred read the paragraph from the *Morning Telegram* and Leon Gonsalez frowned.

"I have an absurd objection to being called a 'gang,' " he said, and Manfred smiled quietly.

"Poor old Falmouth," he reflected, "well, he knows! He was a nice fellow."

"I liked Falmouth," agreed Gonsalez. "He was a perfectly normal man except for a slight progenism – "

Manfred laughed.

"Forgive me if I appear dense, but I have never been able to keep up with you in that particular branch of science," he said, "what is a 'progenism'?"

"The unscientific call it an 'underhung jaw,' " explained Leon, "and it is mistaken for strength. It is only normal in Piedmont where the

37

brachycephalic skull is so common. With such a skull, progenism is almost a natural condition."

"Progenism or not, he was a good fellow," insisted Manfred and Leon nodded. "With well-developed wisdom teeth," he added slyly, and Gonsalez went red, for teeth formed a delicate subject with him. Nevertheless he grinned.

"It will interest you to know, my dear George," he said triumphantly, "that when the famous Dr Carrara examined the teeth of four hundred criminals and a like number of non-criminals – you will find his detailed narrative in the monograph 'Sullo Sviluppo Del Terzo Dente Morale Nei Criminali' – he found the wisdom tooth more frequently present in normal people."

"I grant you the wisdom tooth," said Manfred hastily. "Look at the bay! Did you ever see anything more perfect?"

They were sitting on a little green lawn overlooking Babbacombe Beach. The sun was going down and a perfect day was drawing to its close. High above the blue sea towered the crimson cliffs and green fields of Devon.

Manfred looked at his watch.

"Are we dressing for dinner?" he asked, "or has your professional friend Bohemian tastes?"

"He is of the new school," said Leon, "rather superior, rather immaculate, very Balliol. I am anxious that you should meet him, his hands are rather fascinating."

Manfred in his wisdom did not ask why.

"I met him at golf," Gonsalez went on, "and certain things happened which interested me. For example, every time he saw an earthworm he stopped to kill it and displayed such an extraordinary fury in the assassination that I was astounded. Prejudice has no place in the scientific mind. He is exceptionally wealthy. People at the club told me that his uncle left him close to a million, and the estate of his aunt or cousin who died last year was valued at another million and he was the sole legatee. Naturally a good catch. Whether Miss Moleneux thinks the same I have had no opportunity of gauging," he added after a pause.

"Good lord!" cried Manfred in consternation as he jumped up from his chair. "She is coming to dinner too, isn't she?"

"And her mamma," said Leon solemnly. "Her mamma has learnt Spanish by correspondence lessons, and insists upon greeting me with *habla usted Espanol?*"

The two men had rented Cliff House for the spring. Manfred loved Devonshire in April when the slopes of the hills were yellow with primroses, and daffodils made a golden path across the Devon lawns. "Senor Fuentes" had taken the house after one inspection and found the calm and the peace which only nature's treasury of colour and fragrance could bring to his active mind.

Manfred had dressed and was sitting by the wood fire in the drawing-room when the purr of a motor-car coming cautiously down the cliff road brought him to his feet and through the open French window.

Leon Gonsalez had joined him before the big limousine had come to a halt before the porch.

The first to alight was a man and George observed him closely. He was tall and thin. He was not bad looking, though the face was lined and the eyes deep set and level. He greeted Gonsalez with just a tiny hint of patronage in his tone.

"I hope we haven't kept you waiting, but my experiments detained me. Nothing went right in the laboratory today. You know Miss Moleneux and Mrs Moleneux?"

Manfred was introduced and found himself shaking hands with a grave-eyed girl of singular beauty.

Manfred was unusually sensitive to "atmosphere" and there was something about this girl which momentarily chilled him. Her frequent smile, sweet as it was and undoubtedly sincere, was as undoubtedly mechanical. Leon, who judged people by reason rather than instinct, reached his conclusion more surely and gave shape and definite description to what in Manfred's mind was merely a distressful impression. The girl was afraid! Of what? wondered Leon. Not of that stout, complacent little woman whom she called mother, and surely not of this thin-faced academic gentleman in pince-nez.

Gonsalez had introduced Dr Viglow and whilst the ladies were taking off their cloaks in Manfred's room above, he had leisure to form a judgment. There was no need for him to entertain his guest. Dr Viglow spoke fluently, entertainingly and all the time.

"Our friend here plays a good game of golf," he said, indicating Gonsalez, "a good game of golf indeed for a foreigner. You two are Spanish?"

Manfred nodded. He was more thoroughly English than the doctor, did that gentleman but know, but it was a Spaniard and armed, moreover, with a Spanish passport that he was a visitor to Britain.

"I understand you to say that your investigations have taken rather a sensational turn, Doctor," said Leon and a light came into Dr Viglow's eyes.

"Yes," he said complacently, and then quickly, "who told you that?"

"You told me yourself at the club this morning."

The doctor frowned.

"Did I?" he said and passed his hand across his forehead. "I can't recollect that. When was this?"

"This morning," said Leon, "but your mind was probably occupied with much more important matters."

The young professor bit his lip and frowned thoughtfully.

"I ought not to have forgotten what happened this morning," he said in a troubled tone.

He gave the impression to Manfred that one half of him was struggling desperately to overcome a something in the other half. Suddenly he laughed.

"A sensational turn!" he said. "Yes indeed, and I rather think that within a few months I shall not be without fame, even in my own country! It is, of course, terribly expensive. I was only reckoning up today that my typists' wages come to nearly £60 a week."

Manfred opened his eyes at this.

"Your typists' wages?" he repeated slowly. "Are you preparing a book?"

"Here are the ladies," said Dr Felix.

His manner was abrupt to rudeness and later when they sat round the table in the little dining-room Manfred had further cause to wonder at the boorishness of this young scientist. He was seated next to Miss Moleneux and the meal was approaching its end when most unexpectedly he turned to the girl and in a loud voice said:

"You haven't kissed me today, Margaret."

The girl went red and white and the fingers that fidgeted with the tableware before her were trembling when she faltered:

"Haven't – haven't I, Felix?"

The bright eyes of Gonsalez never left the doctor. The man's face had gone purple with rage.

"By God! This is a nice thing!" he almost shouted. "I'm engaged to you. I've left you everything in my will and I'm allowing your mother a thousand a year and you haven't kissed me today!"

"Doctor!" It was the mild but insistent voice of Gonsalez that broke the tension. "I wonder whether you would tell me what chemical is represented by the formula $C1_2O_5$."

The doctor had turned his head slowly at the sound of Leon's voice and now was staring at him. Slowly the strange look passed from his face and it became normal.

"$C1_2O_5$ is Oxide of Chlorine," he said in an even voice, and from thenceforward the conversation passed by way of acid reactions into a scientific channel.

The only person at the table who had not been perturbed by Viglow's outburst had been the dumpy complacent lady on Manfred's right. She had tittered audibly at the reference to her allowance, and when the hum of conversation became general she lowered her voice and leant toward Manfred.

"Dear Felix is so eccentric," she said, "but he is quite the nicest, kindest soul. One must look after one's girls, don't you agree, senor?"

She asked this latter question in very bad Spanish and Manfred nodded. He shot a glance at the girl. She was still deathly pale.

"And I am perfectly certain she will be happy, much happier than she would have been with that impossible person."

41

She did not specify who the "impossible person" was, but Manfred sensed a whole world of tragedy. He was not romantic, but one look at the girl had convinced him that there was something wrong in this engagement. Now it was that he came to a conclusion which Leon had reached an hour before, that the emotion which dominated the girl was fear. And he pretty well knew of whom she was afraid.

Half an hour later when the tail light of Dr Viglow's limousine had disappeared round a corner of the drive the two men went back to the drawing-room and Manfred threw a handful of kindling to bring the fire to a blaze.

"Well, what do you think?" said Gonsalez, rubbing his hands together with evidence of some enjoyment.

"I think it's rather horrible," replied Manfred, settling himself in his chair. "I thought the days when wicked mothers forced their daughters into unwholesome marriages were passed and done with. One hears so much about the modern girl."

"Human nature isn't modern," said Gonsalez briskly, "and most mothers are fools where their daughters are concerned. I know you won't agree but I speak with authority. Mantegazza collected statistics of 843 families – "

Manfred chuckled.

"You and your Mantegazza!" he laughed. "Did that infernal man know everything?"

"Almost everything," said Leon. "As to the girl," he became suddenly grave. "She will not marry him of course."

"What is the matter with him?" asked Manfred. "He seems to have an ungovernable temper."

"He is mad," replied Leon calmly and Manfred looked at him.

"Mad?" he repeated incredulously. "Do you mean to say that he is a lunatic?"

"I never use the word in a spectacular or even in a vulgar sense," said Gonsalez, lighting a cigarette carefully. "The man is undoubtedly mad. I thought so a few days ago and I am certain of it now. The most ominous test is the test of memory. People who are on the verge of madness or entering its early stages do not remember what happened a short time before. Did you notice how worried he was when I told him of the conversation we had this morning?"

"That struck me as peculiar," agreed Manfred.

"He was fighting," said Leon, "the sane half of his brain against the insane half. The doctor against the irresponsible animal. The doctor told him that if he had suddenly lost his memory for incidents which had occurred only a few hours before, he was on the high way to lunacy. The crazy half of the brain told him that he was such a wonderful fellow that the rules applying to ordinary human beings did not apply to him. We will call upon him tomorrow to see his laboratory and discover why he is paying £60 a week for typists," he said. "And now, my dear George, you can go to bed. I am going to read the excellent but often misguided Lombroso on the male delinquent."

Dr Viglow's laboratory was a new red building on the edge of Dartmoor. To be exact, it consisted of two buildings, one of which was a large army hut which had been recently erected for the accommodation of the doctor's clerical staff.

"I haven't met a professor for two or three years," said Manfred as they were driving across the moor, en route to pay their call, "nor have I been in a laboratory for five. And yet within the space of a few weeks I have met two extraordinary professors, one of whom I admit was dead. Also I have visited two laboratories."

Leon nodded.

"Some day I will make a very complete examination of the phenomena of coincidence," he said.

When they reached the laboratory they found a post-office van, backed up against the main entrance, and three assistants in white overalls were carrying post bags and depositing them in the van.

"He must have a pretty large correspondence," said Manfred in wonder.

The doctor, in a long white overall, was standing at the door as they alighted from their car, and greeted them warmly.

"Come into my office," he said, and led the way to a large airy room which was singularly free from the paraphernalia which Gonsalez usually associated with such work-rooms.

"You have a heavy post," said Leon and the doctor laughed quietly.

"They are merely going to the Torquay post office," he said. "I have arranged for them to be despatched when – " he hesitated, "when I am sure. You see," he said, speaking with great earnestness, "a scientist has to be so careful. Every minute after he has announced a discovery he is tortured with the fear that he has forgotten something, some essential, or has reached a too hasty conclusion. But I think I'm right," he said, speaking half to himself. "I'm sure I'm right, but I must be even more sure!"

He showed them round the large room, but there was little which Manfred had not seen in the laboratory of the late Professor Tableman. Viglow had greeted them genially, indeed expansively, and yet within five minutes of their arrival he was taciturn, almost silent, and did not volunteer information about any of the instruments in which Leon showed so much interest, unless he was asked.

They came back to his room and again his mood changed and he became almost gay.

"I'll tell you," he said, "by Jove, I'll tell you! And no living soul knows this except myself, or realises or understands the extraordinary work I have been doing."

His face lit up, his eyes sparkled and it seemed to Manfred that he grew taller in this moment of exaltation. Pulling open a drawer of a table which stood against the wall he brought out a long porcelain plate and laid it down. From a wire-netted cupboard on the wall he took two tin boxes and with an expression of disgust which he could not disguise, turned the contents upon the slab. It was apparently a box full of common garden mould and then Leon saw to his amazement a wriggling little red shape twisting and twining in its acute discomfort. The little red fellow sought to hide himself and burrowed sinuously into the mould.

"Curse you! Curse you!" The doctor's voice rose until it was a howl. His face was twisted and puckered in his mad rage. "How I hate you!"

If ever a man's eyes held hate and terror, they were the eyes of Dr Felix Viglow.

Manfred drew a long breath and stepped back a pace the better to observe him. Then the man calmed himself and peered down at Leon.

"When I was a child," he said in a voice that shook, "I hated them and we had a nurse named Martha, a beastly woman, a wicked woman, who dropped one down my neck. Imagine the horror of it!"

Leon said nothing. To him the earthworm was a genus of chaetopod in the section *oligochaeta* and bore the somewhat pretentious name of *lumbricus terrestris*. And in that way, Dr Viglow, eminent naturalist and scientist, should have regarded this benificent little fellow.

"I have a theory," said the doctor. He was calmer now and was wiping the sweat from his forehead with a handkerchief, "that in cycles every type of living thing on the earth becomes in turn the dominant creature. In a million years' time man may dwindle to the size of an ant and the earthworm, by its super-intelligence, its cunning and its ferocity, may be pre-eminent in the world! I have always thought that," he went on when neither Leon nor Manfred offered any comment. "It is still my thought by day and my dream by night. I have devoted my life to the destruction of this menace."

Now the earthworm is neither cunning nor intelligent and is moreover notoriously devoid of ambition.

The doctor again went to the cupboard and took out a wide-necked bottle filled with a greyish powder. He brought it back and held it within a few inches of Leon's face.

"This is the work of twelve years," he said simply. "There is no difficulty in finding a substance which will kill these pests, but this does more."

He took a scalpel and tilting the bottle brought out a few grains of the powder on the edge of it. This he dissolved in a twenty-ounce measure which he filled with water. He stirred the colourless fluid

45

with a glass rod, then lifting the rod he allowed three drops to fall upon the mould wherein the little reptile was concealed. A few seconds passed, there was a heaving of the earth where the victim was concealed.

"He is dead," said the doctor triumphantly and scraped away the earth to prove the truth of his words. "And he is not only dead, but that handful of earth is death to any other earthworm that touches it."

He rang a bell and one of his attendants came in.

"Clear away that," he said with a shudder and walked gloomily to his desk.

Leon did not speak all the way back to the house. He sat curled up in the corner of the car, his arms tightly folded, his chin on his breast. That night without a word of explanation he left the house, declining Manfred's suggestion that he should walk with him and volunteering no information as to where he was going.

Gonsalez walked by the cliff road, across Babbacombe Downs and came to the doctor's house at nine o'clock that night. The doctor had a large house and maintained a big staff of servants, but amongst his other eccentricities was the choice of a gardener's cottage away from the house as his sleeping place at night.

It was only lately that the doctor had chosen this lonely lodging. He had been happy enough in the big old house which had been his father's, until he had heard voices whispering to him at night and the creak of boards and had seen shapes vanishing along the dark corridors, and then in his madness he had conceived the idea that his servants were conspiring against him and that he might any night be murdered in his bed. So he had the gardener turned out of his cottage, had refurnished the little house, and there, behind locked doors, he read and thought and slept the nights away. Gonsalez had heard of this peculiarity and approached the cottage with some caution, for a frightened man is more dangerous than a wicked man. He rapped at the door and heard a step across the flagged floor.

"Who is that?" asked a voice.

"It is I," said Gonsalez and gave the name by which he was known.

After hesitation the lock turned and the door opened.

"Come in, come in," said Viglow testily and locked the door behind him. "You have come to congratulate me, I am sure. You must come to my wedding too, my friend. It will be a wonderful wedding, for there I shall make a speech and tell the story of my discovery. Will you have a drink? I have nothing here, but I can get it from the house. I have a telephone in my bedroom."

Leon shook his head.

"I have been rather puzzling out your plan, Doctor," he said, accepting the proffered cigarette, "and I have been trying to connect those postal bags which I saw being loaded at the door of your laboratory with the discovery which you revealed this afternoon."

Dr Viglow's narrow eyes were gleaming with merriment and he leant back in his chair and crossed his legs, like one preparing for a pleasant recital.

"I will tell you," he said. "For months I have been in correspondence with farming associations, both here and on the Continent. I have something of a European reputation," he said, with that extraordinary immodesty which Leon had noticed before. "In fact, I think that my treatment for phylloxera did more to remove the scourge from the vineyards of Europe than any other preparation."

Leon nodded. He knew this to be the truth.

"So you see, my word is accepted in matters dealing with agriculture. But I found after one or two talks with our own stupid farmers that there is an unusual prejudice against destroying" – he did not mention the dreaded name but shivered – "and that of course I had to get round. Now that I am satisfied that my preparation is exact, I can release the packets in the post office. In fact, I was just about to telephone to the postmaster telling him that they could go off – they are all stamped and addressed – when you knocked at the door."

"To whom are they addressed?" asked Leon steadily.

"To various farmers – some fourteen thousand in all in various parts of the country and Europe and each packet has printed instructions in English, French, German and Spanish. I had to tell them that it was a new kind of fertiliser or they may not have been as enthusiastic in the furtherance of my experiment as I am."

"And what are they going to do with these packets when they get them?" asked Leon quietly.

"They will dissolve them and spray a certain area of their land – I suggested ploughed land. They need only treat a limited area of earth," he explained. "I think these wretched beasts will carry infection quickly enough. I believe," he leant forward and spoke impressively, "that in six months there will not be one living in Europe or Asia."

"They do not know that the poison is intended to kill – earthworms?" asked Leon.

"No, I've told you," snapped the other. "Wait, I will telephone the postmaster."

He rose quickly to his feet, but Leon was quicker and gripped his arm.

"My dear friend," he said, "you must not do this."

Dr Viglow tried to withdraw his arm.

"Let me go," he snarled. "Are you one of those devils who are trying to torment me?"

In ordinary circumstances, Leon would have been strong enough to hold the man, but Viglow's strength was extraordinary and Gonsalez found himself thrust back into the chair. Before he could spring up, the man had passed through the door and slammed and locked it behind him.

The cottage was on one floor and was divided into two rooms by a wooden partition which Viglow had erected. Over the door was a fanlight, and pulling the table forward Leon sprang on to the top and with his elbow smashed the flimsy frame.

"Don't touch that telephone," he said sternly. "Do you hear?"

The doctor looked round with a grin.

"You are a friend of those devils!" he said, and his hand was on the receiver when Leon shot him dead.

Manfred came back the next morning from his walk and found Gonsalez pacing the lawn, smoking an extra long cigar.

"My dear Leon," said Manfred as he slipped his arm in the other's. "You did not tell me."

"I thought it best to wait," said Leon.

"I heard quite by accident," Manfred went on. "The story is that a burglar broke into the cottage and shot the doctor when he was telephoning for assistance. All the silverware in the outer room has been stolen. The doctor's watch and pocket-book have disappeared."

"They are at this moment at the bottom of Babbacome Bay," said Leon. "I went fishing very early this morning before you were awake."

They paced the lawn in silence for a while and then:

"Was it necessary?" asked Manfred.

"Very necessary," said Leon gravely. "You have to realise first of all that although this man was mad, he had discovered not only a poison but an infection."

"But, my dear fellow," smiled Manfred, "was an earthworm worth it?"

"Worth more than his death," said Leon. "There isn't a scientist in the world who does not agree that if the earthworm was destroyed the world would become sterile and the people of this world would be starving in seven years."

Manfred stopped in his walk and stared down at his companion.

"Do you really mean that?"

Leon nodded.

"He is the one necessary creature in God's world," he said soberly. "It fertilises the land and covers the bare rocks with earth. It is the surest friend of mankind that we know, and now I am going down to the post office with a story which I think will be sufficiently plausible to recover those worm poisoners."

Manfred mused a while, then he said:

"I'm glad in many ways – in every way," he corrected. "I rather liked that girl, and I'm sure that impossible person isn't so impossible."

THE MAN WHO DIED TWICE

The interval between Acts II and III was an unusually long one, and the three men who sat in the stage box were in such harmony of mind that none of them felt the necessity for making conversation. The piece was a conventional crook play and each of the three had solved the "mystery" of the murder before the drop fell on the first act. They had reached the same solution (and the right one) without any great mental effort.

Fare, the Police Commissioner, had dined with George Manfred and Leon Gonsalez (he addressed them respectively as "Senor Fuentes" and "Senor Mandrelino" and did not doubt that they were natives of Spain, despite their faultless English) and the party had come on to the theatre.

Mr Fare frowned as at some unpleasant memory and heard a soft laugh. Looking up, he met the dancing eyes of Leon.

"Why do you laugh?" he asked, half smiling in sympathy.

"At your thoughts," replied the calm Gonsalez.

"At my thoughts!" repeated the other, startled.

"Yes," Leon nodded, "you were thinking of the Four Just Men."

"Extraordinary!" exclaimed Fare. "It is perfectly true. What is it, telepathy?"

Gonsalez shook his head. As to Manfred, he was gazing abstractedly into the stalls.

"No, it was not telepathy," said Leon, "it was your facial expression."

"But I haven't mentioned those rascals, how – "

"Facial expression," said Leon, revelling in his pet topic, "especially an expression of the emotions, comes into the category of primitive instincts – they are not 'willed'. For example, when a billiard player strikes a ball he throws and twists his body after the ball – you must have seen the contortions of a player who has missed his shot by a narrow margin? A man using scissors works his jaw, a rower moves his lips with every stroke of the oar. These are what we call 'automatisms'. Animals have these characteristics. A hungry dog approaching meat pricks his ears in the direction of his meal – "

"Is there a particular act of automatism produced by the thought of the Four Just Men?" asked the Commissioner, smiling.

Leon nodded.

"It would take long to describe, but I will not deceive you. I less read than guessed your thoughts by following them. That last line in the last act we saw was uttered by a ridiculous stage parson who says: 'Justice! There is a justice beyond the law!' And I saw you frown. And then you looked across the stalls and nodded to the editor of the *Megaphone*. And I remembered that you had written an article on the Four Just Men for that journal – "

"A little biography on poor Falmouth who died the other day," corrected Fare. "Yes, yes, I see. You were right, of course. I was thinking of them and their pretensions to act as judges and executioners when the law fails to punish the guilty, or rather the guilty succeed in avoiding conviction."

Manfred turned suddenly.

"Leon," he spoke in Spanish, in which language the three had been conversing off and on during the evening. "View the cavalier with the diamond in his shirt – what do you make of him?" The question was in English.

Leon raised his powerful opera glasses and surveyed the man whom his friend had indicated.

"I should like to hear him speak," he said after a while. "See how delicate his face is and how powerful are his jaws – almost prognathic for the upper maxilla is distinctly arrested. Regard him, senor, and tell me if you do not agree that his eyes are unusually bright?"

Manfred took the glasses and looked at the unconscious man.

"They are swollen – yes, I see they are bright."

"What else do you see?"

"The lips are large and a little swollen too, I think," said Manfred.

Leon took the glasses and turned to the Commissioner.

"I do not bet, but if I did I would wager a thousand pesetas that this man speaks with a harsh cracked voice."

Fare looked from his companion to the object of their scrutiny and then back to Leon.

"You are perfectly right," he said quietly. "His name is Ballam and his voice is extraordinarily rough and harsh. What is he?"

"Vicious," replied Gonsalez. "My dear friend, that man is vicious, a bad man. Beware of the bright eyes and the cracked voice, senor! They stand for evil!"

Fare rubbed his nose irritably, a trick of his.

"If you were anybody else I should be very rude and say that you knew him or had met him," he said, "but after your extraordinary demonstration the other day I realise there must be something in physiognomy."

He referred to a visit which Leon Gonsalez and Manfred had paid to the record department of Scotland Yard. There, with forty photographs of criminals spread upon the table before him Gonsalez, taking them in order, had enumerated the crimes with which their names were associated. He only made four errors and even they were very excusable.

"Yes, Gregory Ballam is a pretty bad lot," said the Commissioner thoughtfully. "He has never been through our hands, but that is the luck of the game. He's as shrewd as the devil and it hurts me to see him with a nice girl like Genee Maggiore."

"The girl who is sitting with him?" asked Manfred, interested.

"An actress," murmured Gonsalez. "You observe, my dear George, how she turns her head first to the left and then to the right at intervals, though there is no attraction in either direction. She has the habit of being seen – it is not vanity, it is merely a peculiar symptom of her profession."

"What is his favourite vanity?" asked Manfred and the Commissioner smiled.

"You know our Dickens, eh?" he asked, for he thought of Manfred as a Spaniard. "Well, it would be difficult to tell you what Gregory Ballam does to earn his respectable income," he said more seriously. "I think he is connected with a moneylender's business and runs a few profitable sidelines."

"Such as – " suggested Manfred.

Mr Fare was not, apparently, anxious to commit himself.

"I'll tell you in the strictest confidence," he said. "We believe, and have good cause to believe, that he has a hop joint which is frequented by wealthy people. Did you read last week about the man, John Bidworth, who shot a nursemaid in Kensington Gardens and then shot himself?"

Manfred nodded.

"He was quite a well-connected person, wasn't he?" he asked.

"He was very well connected," replied Fare emphatically. "So well connected that we did not want to bring his people into the case at all. He died the next day in hospital and the surgeons tell us that he was undoubtedly under the influence of some Indian drug and that in his few moments of consciousness he as much as told the surgeon in charge of the case that he had been on a jag the night before and had finished up in what he called an opium house and remembered nothing further till he woke up in the hospital. He died without knowing that he had committed this atrocious crime. There is no doubt that under the maddening influence of the drug he shot the first person he saw."

"Was it Mr Ballam's opium house?" asked Gonsalez, interested.

The curtain rose at that moment and conversation went on in a whisper.

"We don't know – in his delirium he mentioned Ballam's name. We have tried our best to find out. He has been watched. Places at which he has stayed any length of time have been visited, but we have found nothing to incriminate him."

Leon Gonsalez had a favourite hour and a favourite meal at which he was at his brightest. That hour was at nine o'clock in the morning and the meal was breakfast. He put down his paper the next morning and asked:

"What is crime?"

"Professor," said Manfred solemnly, "I will tell you. It is the departure from the set rules which govern human society."

"You are conventional," said Gonsalez. "My dear George, you are always conventional at nine o'clock in the morning! Now, had I asked you at midnight you would have told me that it is any act which wilfully offends and discomforts your neighbour. If I desired to give it a narrow and what they call in this country a legal interpretation I would add, 'contrary to the law.' There must be ten thousand crimes committed for every one detected. People associate crime only with those offences which are committed by a certain type of illiterate or semi-illiterate lunatic or half-lunatic, glibly dubbed a 'criminal'. Now, here is a villainous crime, a monumental crime. He is a man who is destroying the souls of youth and breaking hearts ruthlessly! Here is one who is dragging down men and women from the upward road and debasing them in their own eyes, slaying ambition and all beauty of soul and mind in order that he should live in a certain comfort, wearing a clean dress shirt every evening of his life and drinking expensive and unnecessary wines with his expensive and indigestible dinner."

"Where is this man?" asked Manfred.

"He lives at 993 Jermyn Street, in fact he is a neighbour," said Leon.

"You're speaking of Mr Ballam?"

"I'm speaking of Mr Ballam," said Gonsalez gravely. "Tonight I am going to be a foreign artist with large rolls of money in my pockets and an irresistible desire to be amused. I do not doubt that sooner or later Mr Ballam and I will gravitate together. Do I look like a detective, George?" he asked abruptly.

"You look more like a successful pianist," said George and Gonsalez sniffed.

"You can even be offensive at nine o'clock in the morning," he said.

There are two risks which criminals face (with due respect to the opinions of Leon Gonsalez, this word criminal is employed by the narrator) in the pursuit of easy wealth. There is the risk of detection and punishment which applies to the big as well as to the little delinquent. There is the risk of losing large sums of money invested for the purpose of securing even larger sums. The criminal who puts money in his business runs the least risk of detection. That is why only the poor and foolish come stumbling up the stairs which lead to the dock at the Old Bailey, and that is why the big men, who would be indignant at the very suggestion that they were in the category of law-breakers, seldom or never make their little bow to the Judge.

Mr Gregory Ballam stood for and represented certain moneyed interests which had purchased at auction three houses in Montague Street, Portland Place. They were three houses which occupied an island site. The first of these was let out in offices, the ground floor being occupied by a lawyer, the first floor by a wine and spirit merchant, the second being a very plain suite, dedicated to the business hours of Mr Gregory Ballam. This gentleman also rented the cellar, which by the aid of lime-wash and distemper had been converted into, if not a pleasant, at any rate a neat and cleanly storage place. Through this cellar you could reach (amongst other places) a brand-new garage, which had been built for one of Mr Ballam's partners, but in which Mr Ballam was not interested at all.

None but the workmen who had been employed in renovation knew that it was possible also to walk from one house to the other, either through the door in the cellar which had existed when the houses were purchased, or through a new door in Mr Ballam's office.

The third house, that at the end of the island site, was occupied by the International Artists' Club, and the police had never followed Mr Ballam there because Mr Ballam had never gone there, at least not by the front door. The Artists' Club had a "rest room" and there were times when Mr Ballam had appeared, as if by magic, in that room, had met a select little party and conducted them through a well-concealed pass-door to the ground floor of the middle house. The middle house was the most respectable looking of the three. It had neat muslin curtains at all its windows and was occupied by a venerable gentleman and his wife.

The venerable gentleman made a practice of going out to business every morning at ten o'clock, his shiny silk hat set jauntily on the side of his head, a furled umbrella under his arm and a button-hole in his coat. The police knew him by sight and local constables touched their helmets to him. In the days gone by when Mr Raymond, as he called himself, had a luxurious white beard and earned an elegant income by writing begging letters and interviewing credulous and sympathetic females, he did not have that name or the reputation which he enjoyed in Montague Street. But now he was clean-shaven and had the appearance of a retired admiral and he received £4 a week for going out of the house every morning at ten o'clock, with his silk hat set at a rakish angle, and his furled umbrella and his neat little *boutonnière*. He spent most of the day in the Guildhall reading-room and came back at five o'clock in the evening as jaunty as ever.

And his day's work being ended, he and his hard-faced wife went to their little attic room and played cribbage and their language was certainly jaunty but was not venerable.

On the first floor, behind triple black velvet curtains, men and women smoked day and night. It was a large room, being two rooms which had been converted into one and it had been decorated under Mr Ballam's eye. In this room nothing but opium was smoked. If you had a fancy for hasheesh you indulged yourself in a basement apartment. Sometimes Mr Ballam himself came to take a whiff of the dream-herb, but he usually reserved these visits for such occasions as the introduction of a new and profitable client. The pipe had no ill effect upon Mr Ballam. That was his boast. He boasted now to a new client, a rich Spanish artist who had been picked up by one of his jackals and piloted to the International Artists' Club.

"Nor on me," said the newcomer, waving away a yellow-faced Chinaman who ministered to the needs of the smokers. "I always bring my own smoke."

Ballam leant forward curiously as the man took a silver box from his pocket and produced therefrom a green and sticky-looking pill.

"What is that?" asked Ballam curiously.

"It is a mixture of my own, *canabis indica*, opium and a little Turkish tobacco mixed. It is even milder than opium and the result infinitely more wonderful."

"You can't smoke it here," said Ballam, shaking his head. "Try the pipe, old man."

But the "old man" – he was really young in spite of his grey hair – was emphatic.

"It doesn't matter," he said, "I can smoke at home. I only came out of curiosity," and he rose to go.

"Don't be in a hurry," said Ballam hastily. "See here, we've got a basement downstairs where the hemp pipes go – the smokers up here don't like the smell – I'll come down and try one with you. Bring your coffee."

The basement was empty and selecting a comfortable divan Mr Ballam and his guest sat down.

"You can light this with a match, you don't want a spirit stove," said the stranger.

Ballam, sipping his coffee, looked dubiously at the pipe which Gonsalez offered.

"There was a question I was going to ask you," said Leon. "Does running a show like this keep you awake at nights?"

"Don't be silly," said Mr Ballam, lighting his pipe slowly and puffing with evident enjoyment. "This isn't bad stuff at all. Keep me awake at nights? Why should it?"

"Well," answered Leon. "Lots of people go queer here, don't they? I mean it ruins people smoking this kind of stuff."

"That's their look out," said Mr Ballam comfortably. "They get a lot of fun. There's only one life and you've got to die once."

"Some men die twice," said Leon soberly. "Some men who under the influence of a noxious drug go *fantee* and wake to find themselves murderers. There's a drug in the East which the natives call *bal*. It turns men into raving lunatics."

"Well, that doesn't interest me," said Ballam impatiently. "We must hurry up with this smoke. I've a lady coming to see me. Must keep an appointment, old man," he laughed.

"On the contrary, the introduction of this drug into a pipe interests you very much," said Leon, "and in spite of Miss Maggiore's appointment – "

The other stared.

"What the hell are you talking about?" he asked crossly.

"In spite of that appointment I must break the news to you that the drug which turns men into senseless beasts is more potent than any you serve in this den."

"What's it to do with me?" snarled Ballam.

"It interests you a great deal," said Leon coolly, "because you are at this moment smoking a double dose!"

With a howl of rage Ballam sprang to his feet and what happened after that he could not remember. Only something seemed to split in his head, and a blinding light flashed before his eyes and then a whole century of time went past, a hundred years of moving time and an eternity of flashing lights, of thunderous noises, of whispering voices, of ceaseless troubled movement. Sometimes he knew he was talking and listened eagerly to hear what he himself had to say. Sometimes people spoke to him and mocked him and he had a consciousness that he was being chased by somebody.

How long this went on he could not judge. In his half-bemused condition he tried to reckon time but found he had no standard of measurement. It seemed years after that he opened his eyes with a groan, and put his hand to his aching head. He was lying in bed. It was a hard bed and the pillow was even harder. He stared up at the white-washed ceiling and looked round at the plain distempered walls. Then he peered over the side of the bed and saw that the floor was of concrete. Two lights were burning, one above a table and one in a corner of the room where a man was sitting reading a newspaper. He was a curious-looking man and Ballam blinked at him.

"I am dreaming," he said aloud and the man looked up.

"Hello! Do you want to get up?"

Ballam did not reply. He was still staring, his mouth agape. The man was in uniform, in a dark, tight-fitting uniform. He wore a cap on his head and a badge. Round his waist was a shiny black belt and then Ballam read the letters on the shoulder-strap of the tunic.

"AW," he repeated, dazed. "AW."

What did "AW" stand for? And then the truth flashed on him.

Assistant Warder! He glared round the room. There was one window, heavily barred and covered with thick glass. On the wall was pasted a sheet of printed paper. He staggered out of bed and read, still open-mouthed:

"Regulations for His Majesty's Prisons."

He looked down at himself. He had evidently gone to bed with his breeches and stockings on and his breeches were of coarse yellow material and branded with faded black arrows. He was in prison! How long had he been there?

"Are you going to behave today?" asked the warder curtly. "We don't want any more of those scenes you gave us yesterday!"

"How long have I been here?" croaked Ballam.

"You know how long you've been here. You've been here three weeks, yesterday."

"Three weeks!" gasped Ballam. "What is the charge?"

"Now don't come that game with me, Ballam," said the warder, not unkindly. "You know I'm not allowed to have conversations with you. Go back and sleep. Sometimes I think you are as mad as you profess to be."

"Have I been – bad?" asked Ballam.

"Bad?" The warder jerked up his head. "I wasn't in the court with you, but they say you behaved in the dock like a man demented, and when the Judge was passing sentence of death – "

"My God!" shrieked Ballam and fell back on the bed, white and haggard. "Sentenced to death!" He could hardly form the words. "What have I done?"

"You killed a young lady, you know that," said the warder. "I'm surprised at you, trying to come it over me after the good friend I've been to you, Ballam. Why don't you buck up and take your punishment like a man?"

There was a calendar above the place where the warder had been sitting.

"Twelfth of April," read Ballam and could have shrieked again, for it was the first day of March that he met that mysterious stranger. He remembered it all now. *Bal!* The drug that drove men mad.

He sprang to his feet.

"I want to see the Governor! I want to tell them the truth! I've been drugged!"

"Now you've told us all that story before," said the warder with an air of resignation. "When you killed the young lady – "

"What young lady?" shrieked Ballam. "Not Maggiore! Don't tell me – "

"You know you killed her right enough," said the warder. "What's the good of making all this fuss? Now go back to bed, Ballam. You can't do any good by kicking up a shindy this night of all nights in the world."

"I want to see the Governor! Can I write to him?"

"You can write to him if you like," and the warder indicated the table.

Ballam staggered up to the table and sat down shakily in a chair. There was half a dozen sheets of blue notepaper headed in black: "HM Prison, Wandsworth, SW1."

He was in Wandsworth prison! He looked round the cell. It did not look like a cell and yet it did. It was so horribly bare and the door was heavy looking. He had never been in a cell before and of course it was different to what he had expected.

A thought struck him.

"When – when am I to be punished?" he said chokingly.

"Tomorrow!"

The word fell like a sentence of doom and the man fell forward, his head upon his arms and wept hysterically. Then of a sudden he began to write with feverish haste, his face red with weeping.

His letter was incoherent. It was about a man who had come to the club and had given him a drug and then he had spent a whole eternity in darkness seeing lights and being chased by people and hearing whispering voices. And he was not guilty. He loved Genee Maggiore. He would not have hurt a hair of her head.

He stopped here to weep again. Perhaps he was dreaming? Perhaps he was under the influence of this drug. He dashed his knuckles against the wall and the shock made him wince.

"Here, none of that," said the warder sternly. "You get back to bed."

Ballam looked at his bleeding knuckles. It was true! It was no dream! It was true, true!

He lay on the bed and lost consciousness again and when he awoke the warder was still sitting in his place reading. He seemed to doze again for an hour, although in reality it was only for a few minutes, and every time he woke something within him said: "This morning you die!"

Once he sprang shrieking from the bed and had to be thrown back.

"If you give me any more trouble I'll get another officer in and we'll tie you down. Why don't you take it like a man? It's no worse for you than it was for her," said the warder savagely.

After that he lay still and he was falling into what seemed a longer sleep when the warder touched him. When he awoke he found his own clothes laid neatly by the side of the bed upon a chair and he dressed himself hurriedly.

He looked around for something.

"Where's the collar?" he asked trembling.

"You don't need a collar," the warder's voice had a certain quality of sardonic humour.

"Pull yourself together," said the man roughly. "Other people have gone through this. From what I've heard you ran an opium den. A good many of your clients gave us a visit. They had to go through with it, and so must you."

He waited, sitting on the edge of the bed, his face in his hands and then the door opened and a man came in. He was a slight man with a red beard and a mop of red hair.

The warder swung the prisoner round.

"Put your hands behind you," he said and Ballam sweated as he felt the strap grip his wrists.

Then light was extinguished. A cap was drawn over his face and he thought he heard voices behind him. He wasn't fit to die, he knew that. There always was a parson in a case like this. Someone grasped his arm on either side and he walked slowly forward through the door across a yard and through another door. It was a long way and once his knees gave under him but he stood erect. Presently they stopped.

"Stand where you are," said a voice and he found a noose slipped round his neck and waited, waited in agony, minutes, hours it seemed. He took no account of time and could not judge it. Then he heard a heavy step and somebody caught him by the arm.

"What are you doing here, governor?" said a voice.

The bag was pulled from his head. He was in the street. It was night and he stood under the light of a street-lamp. The man regarding him curiously was a policeman.

"Got a bit of rope round your neck, too, somebody tied your hands. What is it – a hold-up case?" said the policeman as he loosened the straps. "Or is it a lark?" demanded the representative of the law.

"I'm surprised at you, an old gentleman like you with white hair!"

Gregory Ballam's hair had been black less than seven hours before when Leon Gonsalez had drugged his coffee and brought him through the basement exit into the big yard at the back of the club.

For here was a nice new garage as Leon had discovered when he prospected the place, and here they were left uninterrupted to play the comedy of the condemned cell with blue sheets of prison notepaper put there for the occasion and a copy of Prison Regulations which was donated quite unwittingly by Mr Fare, Commissioner of Police.

THE MAN WHO HATED AMELIA JONES

There was a letter that came to Leon Gonsalez, and the stamp bore the image and superscription of Alphonse XIII. It was from a placid man who had written his letter in the hour of siesta, when Cordova slept, and he had scribbled all the things which had come into his head as he sat in an orange bower overlooking the lordly Guadalquivir, now in yellow spate.

"It is from Poiccart," said Leon.

"Yes?" replied George Manfred, half asleep in a big armchair before the fire.

That and a green-shaded reading lamp supplied the illumination to their comfortable Jermyn Street flat at the moment.

"And what," said George, stretching himself, "what does our excellent friend Poiccart have to say?"

"A blight has come upon his onions," said Leon solemnly and Manfred chuckled and then was suddenly grave.

There was a time when the name of these three, with one who now lay in the Bordeaux cemetery, had stricken terror to the hearts of evil-doers. In those days the Four Just Men were a menace to the sleep of many cunning men who had evaded the law, yet had not evaded this ubiquitous organisation, which slew ruthlessly in the name of Justice.

Poiccart was growing onions! He sighed and repeated the words aloud.

"And why not?" demanded Leon. "Have you read of the Three Musketeers?"

"Surely," said Manfred, with a smile at the fire.

"In what book, may I ask?" demanded Leon.

"Why, in *The Three Musketeers*, of course," replied Manfred in surprise.

"Then you did wrong," said Leon Gonsalez promptly. "To love the Three Musketeers, you must read of them in *The Iron Mask*. When one of them has grown fat and is devoting himself to his raiment, and one is a mere courtier of the King of France, and the other is old and full of sorrow for his love-sick child. Then they become human, my dear Manfred, just as Poiccart becomes human when he grows onions. Shall I read you bits?"

"Please," said Manfred, properly abashed.

"H'm," read Gonsalez, "I told you about the onions, George. 'I have some gorgeous roses. Manfred would love them...do not take too much heed of this new blood test, by which the American doctor professes that he can detect degrees of relationship...the new little pigs are doing exceedingly well. There is one that is exceptionally intelligent and contemplative. I have named him George.'"

George Manfred by the fire squirmed in his chair and chuckled.

"'This will be a very good year for wine, I am told,'" Leon read on, "'but the oranges are not as plentiful as they were last year...do you know that the fingerprints of twins are identical? Curiously enough the fingerprints of twins of the anthropoid ape are dissimilar. I wish you would get information on this subject...'"

He read on, little scraps of domestic news, fleeting excursions into scientific side-issues, tiny scraps of gossip – they filled ten closely written pages.

Leon folded the letter and put it in his pocket.

"Of course he's not right about the fingerprints of twins being identical. That was one of the illusions of the excellent Lombroso. Anyway the fingerprint system is unsatisfactory."

"I never heard it called into question," said George in surprise. "Why isn't it satisfactory?"

Leon rolled a cigarette with deft fingers, licked down the paper and lit the ragged end before he replied.

"At Scotland Yard, they have, let us say, one hundred thousand fingerprints. In Britain there are fifty million inhabitants. One hundred thousand is exactly one five-hundredth of fifty millions. Suppose you were a police officer and you were called to the Albert Hall where five hundred people were assembled and told that one of these had in his possession stolen property and you received permission to search them. Would you be content with searching one and giving a clean bill to the rest?"

"Of course not," said Manfred, "but I don't see what you mean."

"I mean that until the whole of the country and every country in Europe adopts a system by which every citizen registers his fingerprints and until all the countries have an opportunity of exchanging those fingerprints and comparing them with their own, it is ridiculous to say that no two prints are alike."

"That settles the fingerprint system," said Manfred, *sotto voce.*

"Logically it does," said the complacent Leon, "but actually it will not, of course."

There was a long silence after this and then Manfred reached to a case by the side of the fireplace and took down a book.

Presently he heard the creak of a chair as Gonsalez rose and the soft "pad" of a closing door. Manfred looked up at the clock and, as he knew, it was half past eight.

In five minutes Leon was back again. He had changed his clothing and, as Manfred had once said before, his disguise was perfect. It was not a disguise in the accepted understanding of the word, for he had not in any way touched his face, or changed the colour of his hair. Only by his artistry he contrived to appear just as he wished to appear, an extremely poor man. His collar was clean, but frayed. His boots were beautifully polished, but they were old and patched. He did not permit the crudity of a heel worn down, but had fixed two circular rubber heels just a little too large for their foundations.

"You are an old clerk battling with poverty, and striving to the end to be genteel," said Manfred.

Gonsalez shook his head.

"I am a solicitor who, twenty years ago, was struck off the rolls and ruined because I helped a man to escape the processes of the law. An ever so much more sympathetic rôle, George. Moreover, it brings people to me for advice. One of these nights you must come down to the public bar of the 'Cow and Compasses' and hear me discourse upon the Married Woman's Property Act."

"I never asked you what you were before," said George. "Good hunting, Leon, and my respectful salutations to Amelia Jones!"

Gonsalez was biting his lips thoughtfully and looking into the fire and now he nodded.

"Poor Amelia Jones?" he said softly.

"You're a wonderful fellow," smiled Manfred, "only you could invest a charwoman of middle age with the glamour of romance."

Leon was helping himself to a threadbare overcoat.

"There was an English poet once – it was Pope, I think – who said that everybody was romantic who admired a fine thing, or did one. I rather think Amelia Jones has done both."

The "Cow and Compasses" is a small public-house in Treet Road, Deptford. The gloomy thoroughfare was well-nigh empty, for it was a grey cold night when Leon turned into the bar. The uninviting weather may have been responsible for the paucity of clients that evening, for there were scarcely half a dozen people on the sanded floor when he made his way to the bar and ordered a claret and soda.

One who had been watching for him started up from the deal form on which she had been sitting and subsided again when he walked toward her with glass in hand.

"Well, Mrs Jones," he greeted her, "and how are you this evening?"

She was a stout woman with a white worn face and hands that trembled spasmodically.

"I am glad you've come, sir," she said.

She held a little glass of port in her hand, but it was barely touched. It was on one desperate night when in an agony of terror and fear this woman had fled from her lonely home to the light and comfort of the public-house that Leon had met her. He was at the time pursuing with the greatest caution a fascinating skull which he had seen on the broad shoulders of a Covent Garden porter. He had tracked the owner to his home and to his place of recreation and was beginning to work up to his objective, which was to secure the history and the measurements of this unimaginative bearer of fruit, when the stout charwoman had drifted into his orbit. Tonight she evidently had something on her mind of unusual importance, for she made three lame beginnings before she plunged into the matter which was agitating her.

"Mr Lucas" (this was the name Gonsalez had given to the *habitués* of the "Cow and Compasses"), "I want to ask you a great favour. You've been very kind to me, giving me advice about my husband, and all that. But this is a big favour and you're a very busy gentleman, too."

She looked at him appealingly, almost pleadingly.

"I have plenty of time just now," said Gonsalez.

"Would you come with me into the country tomorrow?" she asked. "I want you to – to – to see somebody."

"Why surely, Mrs Jones," said Gonsalez.

"Would you be at Paddington Station at nine o'clock in the morning. I would pay your fare," she went on fervently. "Of course, I shouldn't allow you to go to any expense – I've got a bit of money put by."

"As to that," said Leon, "I've made a little money myself today, so don't trouble about the fare. Have you heard from your husband?"

"Not from him," she shook her head, "but from another man who has just come out of prison."

Her lips trembled and tears were in her eyes.

"He'll do it, I know he'll do it," she said, with a catch in her voice, "but it's not me that I'm thinking of."

Leon opened his eyes.

"Not you?" he repeated.

He had suspected the third factor, yet he had never been able to fit it in the scheme of this commonplace woman.

"No, sir, not me," she said miserably. "You know he hates me and you know he's going to do me in the moment he gets out, but I haven't told you why."

"Where is he now?" asked Leon.

"Devizes Gaol, he's gone there for his discharge. He'll be out in two months."

"And then he'll come straight to you, you think?"

She shook her head.

"Not he," she said bitterly. "That ain't his way. You don't know him, Mr Lucas. But nobody does know him like I do. If he'd come straight to me it'd be all right, but he's not that kind. He's going to kill me, I tell you, and I don't care how soon it comes. He wasn't called Bash Jones for nothing. I'll get it all right!" she nodded grimly. "He'll just walk into the room and bash me without a word and that'll be the end of Amelia Jones. But I don't mind, I don't mind," she repeated. "It's the other that's breaking my heart and has been all the time."

He knew it was useless to try to persuade her to tell her troubles, and at closing time they left the bar together.

"I'd ask you home only that might make it worse, and I don't want to get you into any kind of bother, Mr Lucas," she said.

He offered his hand. It was the first time he had done so, and she took it in her big limp palm and shook it feebly.

"Very few people have shaken hands with Amelia Jones," thought Gonsalez, and he went back to the flat in Jermyn Street to find Manfred asleep before the fire.

He was waiting at Paddington Station the next morning in a suit a little less shabby, and to his surprise Mrs Jones appeared dressed in better taste than he could have imagined was possible. Her clothes were plain but they effectively disguised the class to which she belonged. She took the tickets for Swindon and there was little conversation on the journey. Obviously she did not intend to unburden her mind as yet.

The train was held up at Newbury whilst a slow up-train shunted to allow a school special to pass. It was crowded with boys and girls who waved a cheery and promiscuous greeting as they passed.

"Of course!" nodded Leon. "It is the beginning of the Easter holidays. I had forgotten."

At Swindon they alighted and then for the first time the woman gave some indication as to the object of their journey.

"We've got to stay on this platform," she said nervously. "I'm expecting to see somebody, and I'd like you to see her, too, Mr Lucas."

Presently another special train ran into the station and the majority of the passengers in this train also were children. Several alighted at the junction, apparently to change for some other destination than London, and Leon was talking to the woman, who he knew was not listening, when he saw her face light up. She left him with a little gasp and walked quickly along the platform to greet a tall, pretty girl wearing the crimson and white hat-ribbon of a famous West of England school.

"Why, Mrs Jones, it is so kind of you to come down to see me. I wish you wouldn't take so much trouble. I should be only too happy to come to London," she laughed. "Is this a friend of yours?"

She shook hands with Leon, her eyes smiling her friendliness.

"It's all right, Miss Grace," said Mrs Jones, agitated. "I just thought I'd pop down and have a look at you. How are you getting on at school, miss?"

"Oh, splendidly," said the girl. "I've won a scholarship."

"Isn't that lovely!" said Mrs Jones in an awe-stricken voice. "You always was wonderful, my dear."

The girl turned to Leon.

"Mrs Jones was my nurse, you know, years and years ago, weren't you, Mrs Jones?"

Amelia Jones nodded.

"How is your husband? Is he still unpleasant?"

"Oh, he ain't so bad, miss," said Mrs Jones bravely. "He's a little trying at times."

"Do you know, I should like to meet him."

"Oh no, you wouldn't, miss," gasped Amelia. "That's only your kind heart. Where are you spending your holidays, miss?" she asked.

"With some friends of mine at Clifton, Molly Walker, Sir George Walker's daughter."

The eyes of Amelia Jones devoured the girl and Leon knew that all the love in her barren life was lavished upon this child she had nursed. They walked up and down the platform together and when her train came in Mrs Jones stood at the carriage door until it drew out from the station and then waited motionless looking after the express until it melted in the distance.

"I'll never see her again!" she muttered brokenly. "I'll never see her again! Oh, my God!"

Her face was drawn and ghastly in its pallor and Leon took her arm.

"You must come and have some refreshment, Mrs Jones. You are very fond of that young lady?"

"Fond of her?" She turned upon him. "Fond of her? She – she is my daughter!"

They had a carriage to themselves going back to Town and Mrs Jones told her story.

"Grace was three years old when her father got into trouble," she said. "He had always been a brute and I think he'd been under the eyes of the police since he was a bit of a kid. I didn't know this when I married him. I was nursemaid in a house that he'd burgled and I was discharged because I'd left the kitchen door ajar for him, not knowing that he was a thief. He did one long lagging and when he came out he swore he wouldn't go back to prison again, and the next time if there was any danger of an alarm being raised, he would make it a case of murder. He and another man got into touch with a rich bookmaker on Blackheath. Bash used to do his dirty work for him, but they quarrelled and Bash and his pal burgled the house and got away with nearly nine thousand pounds.

"It was a big race day and Bash knew there'd be a lot of money in notes that had been taken on the racecourse and that couldn't be traced. I thought he'd killed this man at first. It wasn't his fault that he hadn't. He walked into the room and bashed him as he lay in bed – that was Bash's way – that's how he got his name. He thought there'd be a lot of enquiries and gave me the money to look after. I had to put the notes into an old beer jar half full of sand, ram in the cork and cover the cork and the neck with candle-fat so that the water couldn't get through, and then put it in the cistern which he could reach from one of the upstairs rooms at the back of the house. I was nearly mad with fear because I thought the gentleman had been killed, but I did as I was told and sunk the jar in the cistern. That night Bash and his mate were getting away to the north of England when they were arrested at Euston Station. Bash's friend was killed, for he ran across the line in front of an engine, but they caught Bash and the house was searched from end to end. He got fifteen years' penal servitude and he would have been out two years ago if he hadn't been a bad character in prison.

"When he was in gaol I had to sit down and think, Mr Lucas, and my first thought was of my child. I saw the kind of life that she was going to grow up to, the surroundings, the horrible slums, the fear of the police, for I knew that Bash would spend a million if he had it in a few weeks. I knew I was free of Bash for at least twelve years and I thought and I thought and at last I made up my mind.

"It was twelve months after he was in gaol that I dared get the money, for the police were still keeping their eye on me as the money had not been found. I won't tell you how I bought grand clothes so that nobody would suspect I was a working woman or how I changed the money.

"I put it all into shares. I'm not well educated, but I read the newspapers for months, the columns about money. At first I was puzzled and I could make no end to it, but after a while I got to understand and it was in an Argentine company that I invested the money, and I got a lawyer in Bermondsey to make a trust of it. She gets the interest every quarter and pays her own bills – I've never touched a penny of it. The next thing was to get my little girl out of the neighbourhood, and I sent her away to a home for small children – it broke my heart to part with her – until she was old enough to go into a school. I used to see her regularly and when, after my first visit,

I found she had almost forgotten who I was, I pretended that I'd been her nurse – and that's the story."

Gonsalez was silent.

"Does your husband know?"

"He knows I spent the money," said the woman, staring blankly out of the window. "He knows that the girl is at a good school. He'll find out," she spoke almost in a whisper. "He'll find out!"

So that was the tragedy! Leon was struck dumb by the beauty of this woman's sacrifice. When he found his voice again, he asked:

"Why do you think he will kill you? These kind of people threaten."

"Bash doesn't threaten as a rule," she interrupted him. "It's the questions he's been asking people who know me. People from Deptford who he's met in prison. Asking what I do at nights, what time I go to bed, what I do in the daytime. That's Bash's way."

"I see," said Leon. "Has anybody given him the necessary particulars?" he asked.

She shook her head.

"They've done their best for me," she said. "They are bad characters and they commit crimes, but there's some good hearts amongst them. They have told him nothing."

"Are you sure?"

"I'm certain. If they had he wouldn't be still asking. Why, Toby Brown came up from Devizes a month ago and told me Bash was there and was still asking questions about me. He'd told Toby that he'd never do another lagging and that he reckoned he'd be alive up to Midsummer Day if they caught him."

Leon went up to his flat that night exalted.

"What have you been doing with yourself?" asked Manfred. "I for my part have been lunching with the excellent Mr Fare."

"And I have been moving in a golden haze of glory! Not my own, no, not my own, Manfred," he shook his head, "but the glory of Amelia Jones. A wonderful woman, George. For her sake I am going to take a month's holiday, during which time you can go back to Spain and see our beloved Poiccart and hear all about the onions."

"I would like to go back to Madrid for a few days," said Manfred thoughtfully. "I find London particularly attractive, but if you really are going to take a holiday – where are you spending it, by the way?"

"In Devizes Gaol," replied Gonsalez cheerfully, and Manfred had such faith in his friend that he offered no comment.

Leon Gonsalez left for Devizes the next afternoon. He arrived in the town at dusk and staggered unsteadily up the rise toward the market-place. At ten o'clock that night a police constable found him leaning against a wall at the back of the Bear Hotel, singing foolish songs, and ordered him to move away. Whereupon Leon addressed him in language for which he was at the time (since he was perfectly sober) heartily ashamed. Therefore he did appear before a bench of magistrates the next morning, charged with being drunk, using abusive language and obstructing the police in the execution of their duty.

"This is hardly a case which can be met by imposing a fine," said the staid chairman of the Bench. "Here is a stranger from London who comes into this town and behaves in a most disgusting manner. Is anything known against the man?"

"Nothing, sir," said the gaoler regretfully.

"You will pay a fine of twenty shillings or go to prison for twenty-one days."

"I would much rather go to prison than pay," said Leon truthfully.

So they committed him to the local gaol as he had expected. Twenty-one days later, looking very brown and fit, he burst into the flat and Manfred turned with outstretched hands.

"I heard you were back," said Leon joyously. "I've had a great time! They rather upset my calculations by giving me three weeks instead of a month, and I was afraid that I'd get back before you."

"I came back yesterday," said George and his eyes strayed to the sideboard.

Six large Spanish onions stood in a row and Leon Gonsalez doubled up with mirth. It was not until he had changed into more presentable garments that he told of his experience.

"Bash Jones had undoubtedly homicidal plans," he said. "The most extraordinary case of facial anamorphosis I have seen. I worked with him in the tailor's shop. He is coming out next Monday."

"He welcomed you, I presume, when he discovered you were from Deptford?" said Manfred dryly.

Leon nodded.

"He intends to kill his wife on the third of the month, which is the day after he is released," he said.

"Why so precise?" asked Manfred in surprise.

"Because that is the only night she sleeps in the house alone. There are usually two young men lodgers who are railwaymen and these do duty until three in the morning on the third of every month."

"Is this the truth or are you making it up?" asked Manfred.

"I did make it up," admitted Gonsalez. "But this is the story I told and he swallowed it eagerly. The young men have no key, so they come in by the kitchen door which is left unlocked. The kitchen door is reached by a narrow passage which runs the length of Little Mill Street and parallel with the houses. Oh yes, he was frightfully anxious to secure information, and he told me that he would never come back to gaol again except for a short visit. An interesting fellow. I think he had better die," said Leon, with some gravity. "Think of the possibilities for misery, George. This unfortunate girl, happy in her friends, well-bred – "

"Would you say that," smiled Manfred, "with Bash for a father?"

"Well-bred, I repeat," said Gonsalez firmly. "Breeding is merely a quality acquired through life-long association with gentle-folk. Put the son of a duke in the slums and he'll grow up a peculiar kind of slum child, but a slum child nevertheless. Think of the horror of it. Dragging this child back to the kennels of Deptford, for that will be the meaning of it, supposing this Mr Bash Jones does not kill his wife. If he kills her then the grisly truth is out. No, I think we had better settle this Mr Bash Jones."

"I agreed," said Manfred, puffing thoughtfully at his cigar, and Leon Gonsalez sat down at the table with Browning's poems open before him and read, pausing now and again to look thoughtfully into space as he elaborated the method by which Bash Jones should die.

On the afternoon of the third, Mrs Amelia Jones was called away by telegram. She met Leon Gonsalez at Paddington Station.

"You have brought your key with you, Mrs Jones?"

"Yes, sir," said the woman in surprise, then, "Do you know that my husband is out of prison?"

"I know, I know," said Gonsalez, "and because he is free I want you to go away for a couple of nights. I have some friends in Plymouth. They will probably meet you at the station and if they do not meet you, you must go to this address."

He gave her an address of a boarding-house that he had secured from a Plymouth newspaper.

"Here is some money. I insist upon your taking it. My friends are very anxious to help you."

She was in tears when he left her.

"You are sure you have locked up your house?" said Leon at parting.

"I've got the key here, sir."

She opened her bag and he noticed that now her hands trembled all the time.

"Let me see," said Leon, taking the bag in his hand and peering at the interior in his short-sighted way. "Yes, there it is."

He put in his hand, brought it out apparently empty and closed the bag again.

"Goodbye, Mrs Jones," he said, "and don't lose courage."

When dark fell Leon Gonsalez arrived in Little Mill Street carrying a bulky something in a black cloth bag. He entered the house unobserved, for the night was wet and gusty and Little Mill Street crouched over its scanty fires.

He closed the door behind him and with the aid of his pocket lamp found his way to the one poor bedroom in the tiny house. He turned down the cover, humming to himself, then very carefully he removed the contents of the bag, the most important of which was a large glass globe.

Over this he carefully arranged a black wig and searched the room for articles of clothing which might be rolled into the bundle. When he had finished his work, he stepped back and regarded it with admiration. Then he went downstairs, unlocked the kitchen door, and to make absolutely certain crossed the little yard and examined the fastening of the gate which led from the lane. The lock apparently was permanently out of order and he went back satisfied.

In one corner of the room was a clothes hanger, screened from view by a length of cheap cretonne. He had cleared this corner of its clothing to make up the bundle on the bed. Then he sat down in a chair and waited with the patience which is the peculiar attribute of the scientist.

The church bells had struck two when he heard the back gate creak, and rising noiselessly took something from his pocket and stepped behind the cretonne curtain. It was not a house in which one could move without sound, for the floorboards were old and creaky and every stair produced a creak. But the man who was creeping from step to step was an artist and Leon heard no other sound until the door slowly opened and a figure came in.

It moved with stealthy steps across the room and stood for a few seconds by the side of the bulky figure in the bed. Apparently he listened and was satisfied. Then Leon saw a stick rise and fall.

Bash Jones did not say a word until he heard the crash of the broken glass. Then he uttered an oath and Leon heard him fumble in his pocket for his matches. The delay was fatal. The chlorine gas, compressed at a pressure of many atmospheres, surged up around him. He choked, turned to run and fell, and the yellow gas rolled over him in a thick and turgid cloud.

Leon Gonsalez stepped from his place of concealment and the dying man staring up saw two enormous glass eyes and the snout-like nozzle of the respirator and went bewildered to his death.

Leon collected the broken glass and carefully wrapped the pieces in his bag. He replaced the clothes with the most extraordinary care and put away the wig and tidied the room before he opened the window and the door. Then he went to the front of the house and opened those windows too. A south-wester was blowing and by the morning the house would be free from gas.

Not until he was in the back yard did he remove the gas mask he wore and place that too in the bag.

An hour later he was in his own bed in a deep, untroubled sleep.

Mrs Jones slept well that night, and in a dainty cubicle somewhere in the west of England a slim girlish figure in pyjamas snuggled into her pillow and sighed happily.

But Bash Jones slept soundest of all.

THE MAN WHO WAS HAPPY

On a pleasant evening in early summer, Leon Gonsalez descended from the top of a motor-omnibus at Piccadilly Circus and walking briskly down the Haymarket, turned into Jermyn Street apparently oblivious of the fact that somebody was following on his heels.

Manfred looked up from his writing as his friend came in, and nodded smilingly as Leon took off his light overcoat and made his way to the window overlooking the street.

"What are you searching for so anxiously, Leon?" he asked.

"Jean Prothero, of 75 Barside Buildings, Lambeth," said Leon, not taking his eyes from the street below. "Ah, there he is, the industrious fellow!"

"Who is Jean Prothero?"

Gonsalez chuckled.

"A very daring man," evaded Leon, "to wander about the West End at this hour." He looked at his watch. "Oh no, not so daring," he said, "everybody who is anybody is dressing for dinner just now."

" A ladder larcenist?" suggested Manfred, and Leon chuckled again.

"Nothing so vulgar," he said. "By ladder larcenist I presume you mean the type of petty thief who puts a ladder against a bedroom window whilst the family are busy at dinner downstairs, and makes off with the odd scraps of jewellery he can find?"

Manfred nodded.

"That is the official description of this type of criminal," he agreed.

Leon shook his head.

"No, Mr Prothero is interesting," he said. "Interesting for quite another reason. In the first place, he is a bald-headed criminal, or potential criminal, and as you know, my dear George, criminals are rarely bald. They are coarse-haired, and they are thin-haired: they have such personal eccentricities as parting their hair on the wrong side, but they are seldom bald. The dome of Mr Prothero's head is wholly innocent of hair of any kind. He is the second mate of a tramp steamer engaged in the fruit trade between the Canary Islands and Southampton. He has a very pretty girl for a wife and, curiously enough, a ladder larcenist for a brother-in-law, and I have excited his suspicion quite unwittingly. Incidentally," he added as though it were a careless afterthought, "he knows that I am one of the Four Just Men."

Manfred was silent. Then:

"How does he know that?" he asked quietly.

Leon had taken off his coat and had slipped his arms into a faded alpaca jacket; he did not reply until he had rolled and lit an untidy Spanish cigarette.

"Years ago, when there was a hue and cry after that pernicious organisation, whose name I have mentioned, an organisation which, in its humble way, endeavoured to right the injustice of the world and to mete out to evil-doers the punishment which the ponderous machinery of the Law could not inflict, you were arrested, my dear George, and consigned to Chelmsford Gaol. From there you made a miraculous escape, and reaching the coast you and I and Poiccart were taken aboard the yacht of our excellent friend the Prince of the Asturias, who honoured us by acting as the fourth of our combination."

Manfred nodded.

"On the ship was Mr Jean Prothero," said Leon. "How he came to be on the yacht of His Serene Highness I will explain at a later stage, but assuredly he was there. I never forget faces, George, but unfortunately I am not singular in this respect, Mr Prothero remembered me, and seeing me in Barside Buildings – "

"What were you doing in Barside Buildings?" asked Manfred with a faint smile.

"In Barside Buildings," replied Leon impressively, "are two men unknown to one another, both criminals, and both colour-blind!"

Manfred put down his pen and turned, prepared for a lecture on criminal statistics, for he had noticed the enthusiasm in Gonsalez's voice.

"By means of these two men," said Leon joyously, "I am able to refute the perfectly absurd theories which both Mantegazza and Scheml have expounded, namely, that criminals are never colour-blind. The truth is, my dear George, both these men have been engaged in crime since their early youth. Both have served terms of imprisonment, and what is more important, their fathers were colour-blind and criminals!"

"Well, what about Mr Prothero?" said Manfred, tactfully interrupting what promised to be an exhaustive disquisition upon optical defects in relation to congenital lawlessness.

"One of my subjects is Prothero's brother-in-law, or rather, half-brother to Mrs Prothero, her own father having been a blameless carpenter, and lives in the flat overhead. These flats are just tiny dwelling places consisting of two rooms and a kitchen. The builders of Lambeth tenements do not allow for the luxury of a bathroom. In this way I came to meet Mrs Prothero whilst overcoming the reluctance of her brother to talk about himself."

"And you met Prothero, too, I presume," said Manfred patiently.

"No, I didn't meet him, except by accident. He passed on the stairs and I saw him give me a swift glance. His face was in the shadow and I did not recognise him until our second meeting, which was today. He followed me home. As a matter of fact," he added, "I have an idea that he followed me yesterday, and only came today to confirm my place of residence."

"You're a rum fellow," said Manfred.

"Maybe I'll be rummer," smiled Leon. "Everything depends now," he said thoughtfully, "upon whether Prothero thinks that I recognised him. If he does – "

Leon shrugged his shoulders.

"Not for the first time have I fenced with death and overcome him," he said lightly.

Manfred was not deceived by the flippancy of his friend's tone.

"As bad as that, eh?" he said, "and more dangerous for him, I think," he added quietly. "I do not like the idea of killing a man because he has recognised us – that course does not seem to fit in with my conception of justice."

"Exactly," said Leon briskly, "and there will be no need, I think. Unless, of course – " he paused.

"Unless what?" asked Manfred.

"Unless Prothero really does love his wife, in which case it may be a very serious business."

The next morning he strolled into Manfred's bedroom carrying the cup of tea which the servant usually brought, and George stared at him in amazement.

"What is the matter with you, Leon, haven't you been to bed?"

Leon Gonsalez was dressed in what he called his "pyjama outfit" – a grey flannel coat and trousers, belted at the waist, a silk shirt open at the neck and a pair of light slippers constituted his attire, and Manfred, who associated this costume with all-night studies, was not astonished when Leon shook his head.

"I have been sitting in the dining-room, smoking the pipe of peace," he said.

"All night?" said Manfred in surprise. "I woke up in the middle of the night and I saw no light."

"I sat in the dark," admitted Leon. "I wanted to hear things."

Manfred stirred his tea thoughtfully. "Is it as bad as that? Did you expect – " Leon smiled.

"I didn't expect what I got," he said. "Will you do me a favour, my dear George?"

"What is your favour?"

"I want you not to speak of Mr Prothero for the rest of the day. Rather, I wish you to discuss purely scientific and agricultural matters, as becomes an honest Andalusian farmer, and moreover to speak in Spanish."

Manfred frowned.

"Why?" and then: "I'm sorry, I can't get out of the habit of being mystified, you know, Leon. Spanish and agriculture it shall be, and no reference whatever to Prothero."

Leon was very earnest and Manfred nodded and swung out of bed.

"May I talk of taking a bath?" he asked sardonically.

Nothing particularly interesting happened that day. Once Manfred was on the point of referring to Leon's experience, and divining the drift of his thought, Leon raised a warning finger.

Gonsalez could talk about crime, and did. He talked of its more scientific aspects and laid particular stress upon his discovery of the colour-blind criminal. But of Mr Prothero he said no word.

After they had dined that night, Leon went out of the flat and presently returned.

"Thank heaven we can now talk without thinking," he said.

He pulled a chair to the wall and mounted it nimbly. Above his head was a tiny ventilator fastened to the wall with screws. Humming a little tune he turned a screwdriver deftly and lifted the little grille from its socket, Manfred watching him gravely.

"Here it is," said Leon. "Pull up a chair, George."

"It" proved to be a small flat brown box four inches by four in the centre of which was a black vulcanite depression.

"Do you recognise him?" said Leon. "He is the detectaphone – in other words a telephone receiver fitted with a microphonic attachment."

"Has somebody been listening to all we've been saying?"

Leon nodded.

"The gentleman upstairs has had a dull and dreary day. Admitting that he speaks Spanish, and that I have said nothing which has not illuminated that branch of science which is my particular hobby," he added modestly, "he must have been terribly bored."

"But – " began Manfred.

"He is out now," said Gonsalez. "But to make perfectly sure – "

With deft fingers he detached one of the wires by which the box was suspended in the ventilator shaft.

"Mr Prothero came last night," he explained. "He took the room upstairs, and particularly asked for it. This I learnt from the head waiter – he adores me because I give him exactly three times the tip which he gets from other residents in these service flats, and because I tip him three times as often. I didn't exactly know what Prothero's game was, until I heard the tap-tap of the microphone coming down the shaft."

He was busy re-fixing the grille of the ventilator – presently he jumped down.

"Would you like to come to Lambeth today? I do not think there is much chance of our meeting Mr Prothero. On the other hand, we shall see Mrs Prothero shopping at eleven o'clock in the London Road, for she is a methodical lady."

"Why do you want to see her?" asked Manfred.

He was not usually allowed to see the workings of any of Leon's schemes until the dramatic dénouement, which was meat and drink to him, was near at hand.

"I want you, with your wide knowledge of human nature, to tell me whether she is the type of woman for whom a bald-headed man would commit murder," he said simply, and Manfred stared at him in amazement.

"The victim being – ?"

"Me!" replied Gonsalez, and doubled up with silent laughter at the blank look on Manfred's face.

It was four minutes to eleven exactly when Manfred saw Mrs Prothero. He felt the pressure of Leon's hand on his arm and looked.

"There she is," said Leon.

A girl was crossing the road. She was neatly, even well-dressed for one of her class. She carried a market bag in one gloved hand, a purse in the other.

"She's pretty enough," said Manfred.

The girl had paused to look in a jeweller's window and Manfred had time to observe her. Her face was sweet and womanly, the eyes big and dark, the little chin firm and rounded.

"What do you think of her?" said Leon.

"I think she's rather a perfect specimen of young womanhood," said Manfred.

"Come along and meet her," said the other, and took his arm.

The girl looked round at first in surprise, and then with a smile. Manfred had an impression of flashing white teeth and scarlet lips parted in amusement. Her voice was not the voice of a lady, but it was quiet and musical.

"Good morning, Doctor," she said to Leon. "What are you doing in this part of the world so early in the morning?"

"Doctor," noted Manfred.

The adaptable Gonsalez assumed many professions for the purpose of securing his information.

"We have just come from Guy's Hospital. This is Dr Selbert," he introduced Manfred. "You are shopping, I suppose?"

She nodded.

"Really, there was no need for me to come out, Mr Prothero being away at the Docks for three days," she replied.

"Have you seen your brother this morning?" asked Leon.

A shadow fell over the girl's face.

"No," she said shortly.

Evidently, thought Manfred, she was not particularly proud of her relationship. Possibly she suspected his illicit profession, but at any rate she had no desire to discuss him, for she changed the subject quickly.

They talked for a little while, and then with an apology she left them and they saw her vanish through the wide door of a grocer's store.

"Well, what do you think of her?"

"She is a very beautiful girl," said Manfred quietly.

"The kind of girl that would make a bald-headed criminal commit a murder?" asked Leon, and Manfred laughed.

"It is not unlikely," he said, "but why should he murder you?"

"*Nous verrons*," replied Leon.

When they returned to their flat in the afternoon the mail had been and there were half a dozen letters. One bearing a heavy crest upon the envelope attracted Manfred's attention.

"Lord Pertham," he said, looking at the signature. "Who is Lord Pertham?"

"I haven't a *Who's Who* handy, but I seem to know the name," said Leon. "What does Lord Pertham want?"

"I'll read you the note," said Manfred. " 'Dear Sir,' " it read.

" 'Our mutual friend of Mr Fare of Scotland Yard is dining with us tonight at Connaught Gardens, and I wonder whether you would come along? Mr Fare tells me that you are one of the cleverest criminologists of the century, and as it is a study which I have made particularly my own, I shall be glad to make your acquaintance.' "

It was signed "Pertham" and there was a postscript running –

"Of course, this invitation also includes your friend."

Manfred rubbed his chin.

"I really do not want to dine fashionably tonight," he said.

"But I do," said Leon promptly. "I have developed a taste for English cooking, and I seem to remember that Lord Pertham is an epicurean."

Promptly at the hour of eight they presented themselves at the big house standing at the corner of Connaught Gardens and were admitted by a footman who took their hats and coats and showed them into a large and gloomy drawing-room.

A man was standing with his back to the fire – a tall man of fifty with a mane of grey hair, that gave him an almost leonine appearance.

He came quickly to meet them.

"Which is Mr Fuentes?" he asked, speaking in English.

"I am Signor Fuentes," replied Manfred, with a smile, "but it is my friend who is the criminologist."

"Delighted to meet you both – but I have an apology to make to you," he said, speaking hurriedly. "By some mischance – the stupidity of one of my men – the letter addressed to Fare was not posted. I only discovered it half an hour ago. I hope you don't mind."

Manfred murmured something conventional and then the door opened to admit a lady.

"I want to present you to her ladyship," said Lord Pertham.

The woman who came in was thin and vinegary, a pair of pale eyes, a tight-lipped mouth and a trick of frowning deprived her of whatever charm Nature had given to her.

Leon Gonsalez, who analysed faces automatically and mechanically, thought, "Spite – suspicion – uncharity – vanity."

The frown deepened as she offered a limp hand.

"Dinner is ready, Pertham," she said, and made no attempt to be agreeable to her guests.

It was an awkward meal. Lord Pertham was nervous and his nervousness might have communicated itself to the two men if they had been anything but what they were. This big man seemed to be in terror of his wife – was deferential, even humble in her presence, and when at last she swept her sour face from the room he made no attempt to hide his sigh of relief.

"I am afraid we haven't given you a very good dinner," he said. "Her ladyship has had a little – er – disagreement with my cook."

Apparently her ladyship was in the habit of having little disagreements with her cook, for in the course of the conversation which followed he casually mentioned certain servants in his household who were no longer in his employ. He spoke mostly of their facial characteristics, and it seemed to Manfred, who was listening as intently as his companion, that his lordship was not a great authority on the subject. He spoken haltingly, made several obvious slips, but Leon did not correct him. He mentioned casually that he had an additional interest in criminals because his own life had been threatened.

"Let us go up and join my lady," he said after a long and blundering exposition of some phase of criminology which Manfred could have sworn he had read up for the occasion.

They went up the broad stairs into a little drawing-room on the first floor. It was empty. His lordship was evidently surprised.

"I wonder – " he began, when the door opened and Lady Pertham ran in. Her face was white and her thin lips were trembling.

"Pertham," she said rapidly, "I'm sure there's a man in my dressing-room."

"In your dressing-room?" said Lord Pertham, and ran out quickly.

The two men would have followed him, but he stopped halfway up the stairs and waved them back.

"You had better wait with her ladyship," he said. "Ring for Thomas, my love," he said.

Standing at the foot of the stairs they heard him moving about. Presently they heard a cry and the sound of a struggle. Manfred was halfway up the stairs when a door slammed above. Then came the sound of voices and a shot, followed by a heavy fall.

Manfred flung himself against the door from whence the sound came.

"It's all right," said Lord Pertham's voice.

A second later he unlocked the door and opened it.

"I'm afraid I've killed this fellow."

The smoking revolver was still in his hand. In the middle of the floor lay a poorly dressed man and his blood stained the pearl-grey carpet.

Gonsalez walked quickly to the body and turned it over. At the first sight he knew that the man was dead. He looked long and earnestly in his face, and Lord Pertham said:

"Do you know him?"

"I think so," said Gonsalez quietly. "He is my colour-blind criminal," for he had recognised the brother of Mrs Prothero.

They walked home to their lodgings that night leaving Lord Pertham closeted with a detective-inspector, and Lady Pertham in hysterics.

Neither man spoke until they reached their flat, then Leon, with a sigh of content, curled up in the big armchair and pulled lovingly at an evil-smelling cigar.

"Leon!"

He took no notice.

"Leon!"

Leon shifted his head round and met George's eye.

"Did anything about that shooting tonight strike you as peculiar?"

"Several things," said Leon.

"Such as?"

"Such as the oddness of the fate that took Slippery Bill – that was the name of my burglar – to Lord Pertham's house. It was not odd that he should commit the burglary, because he was a ladder larcenist, as you call him. By the way, did you look at the dead man's hand?" he asked, twisting round and peering across the table at Manfred.

"No, I didn't," said the other in surprise.

"What a pity – you would have thought it still more peculiar. What are the things you were thinking of?"

"I was wondering why Lord Pertham carried a revolver. He must have had it in his pocket at dinner."

"That is easily explained," said Gonsalez. "Don't you remember his telling us that his life had been threatened in anonymous letters?"

Manfred nodded.

"I had forgotten that," he said. "But who locked the door?"

"The burglar, of course," said Leon and smiled. And by that smile Manfred knew that he was prevaricating. "And talking of locked doors – " and rose.

He went into his room and returned with two little instruments that looked like the gongs of electric bells, except that there was a prong sticking up from each.

He locked the sitting-room door and placed one of these articles on the floor, sticking the spike into the bottom of the door so that it was impossible to open without exercising pressure upon the bell. He tried it and there was a shrill peal.

"That's all right," he said, and turned to examine the windows.

"Are you expecting burglars?"

"I am rather," said Leon, "and really I cannot afford to lose my sleep."

Not satisfied with the fastening of the window he pushed in a little wedge, and performed the same office to the second of the windows looking upon the street.

Another door, leading to Manfred's room from the passage without, he treated as he had served the first.

In the middle of the night there was a frantic ring from one of the bells. Manfred leapt out of bed and switched on the light. His own door was fast and he raced into the sitting-room, but Gonsalez was there before him examining the little sentinel by the door. The door had been unlocked. He kicked away the alarm with his slippered foot.

"Come in, Lord Pertham," he said. "Let's talk this matter over."

There was a momentary silence, then the sound of a slippered foot, and a man came in. He was fully dressed and hatless, and Manfred, seeing the bald head, gasped.

"Sit down and make yourself at home, and let me relieve you of that lethal weapon you have in your pocket, because this matter can be arranged very amicably," said Leon.

It was undoubtedly Lord Pertham, though the great mop of hair had vanished, and Manfred could only stare as Leon's left hand slipped into the pocket of the midnight visitor and drew forth a revolver which he placed carefully on the mantelshelf.

Lord Pertham sank into a chair and covered his face with his hands. For a while the silence was unbroken.

"You may remember the Honourable George Fearnside," began Leon, and Manfred started.

"Fearnside? Why, he was on the Prince's yacht – "

"He was on the Prince's yacht," agreed Gonsalez, "and we thoroughly believed that he did not associate us with escaping malefactors, but apparently he knew us for the Four Just Men. You came into your title about six years ago, didn't you, Pertham?"

The bowed figure nodded. Presently he sat up – his face was white and there were black circles about his eyes.

"Well, gentlemen," he said, "it seems that instead of getting you, you have got me. Now what are you going to do?"

Gonsalez laughed softly.

"For myself," he said, "I am certainly not going in the witness-box to testify that Lord Pertham is a bigamist and for many years has been leading a double life. Because that would mean I should also have to admit certain uncomfortable things about myself."

The man licked his lips and then:

"I came to kill you," he said thickly.

"So we gather," said Manfred. "What is this story, Leon?"

"Perhaps his lordship will tell us," said Gonsalez.

Lord Pertham looked round for something.

"I want a glass of water," he said, and it was Leon who brought it.

"It is perfectly true," said Lord Pertham after a while. "I recognised you fellows as two of the Four Just Men. I used to be a great friend of His Highness, and it was by accident that I was on board the yacht when you were taken off. His Highness told me a yarn about some escapade, but when I got to Spain and read the newspaper account of the escape I was pretty certain that I knew who you were. You probably know something about my early life, how I went before the mast as a common sailor and travelled all over the world. It was the kind of life which satisfied me more than any other, for I got to know people and places and to know them from an angle which I should never have understood in any other way. If you ever want to see the world, travel in the fo'c'sle," he said with a half smile.

"I met Martha Grey one night in the East End of London at a theatre. When I was a seaman I acted like a seaman. My father and I were not on the best of terms and I never wanted to go home. She sat by my side in the pit of the theatre and ridiculous as it may seem to you I fell in love with her."

"You were then married?" said Leon, but the man shook his head.

"No," he said quickly. "Like a fool I was persuaded to marry her ladyship about three months later, after I had got sick of the sea and had come back to my own people. She was an heiress and it was a good match for me. That was before my father had inherited his cousin's money. My life with her ladyship was a hell upon earth. You saw her tonight and you can guess the kind of woman she is. I have too great a respect for women and live too much in awe of them to exercise any control over her viperish temper and it was the miserable life I lived with her which drove me to seek out Martha.

"Martha is a good girl," he said, and there was a glitter in his eye as he challenged denial. "The purest, the dearest, the sweetest woman that ever lived. It was when I met her again that I realised how deeply in love I was, and as with a girl of her character there was no other way – I married her. I had fever when I was on a voyage to Australia and lost all my hair. That was long before I met Martha. I suppose it was vanity on my part, but when I went back to my own life and my own people, as I did for a time after that, I had a wig made which served the double purpose of concealing my infirmity and preventing my being recognised by my former shipmates.

"As the little hair I had had gone grey I had the wig greyed too, had it made large and poetical – " he smiled sadly, "to make my disguise more complete. Martha didn't mind my bald head, God bless her!" he said softly, "and my life with her has been a complete and unbroken period of happiness. I have to leave her at times to manage my own affairs and in those times I pretend to be at sea, just as I used to pretend to her ladyship that business affairs called me to America to explain my absence from her."

"The man you shot was Martha's half-brother, of course," said Gonsalez, and Lord Pertham nodded.

"It was just ill luck which brought him to my house," he said, "sheer bad luck. In the struggle my wig came off, he recognised me and I shot him," he said simply. "I shot him deliberately and in cold blood, not only because he threatened to wreck my happiness, but because for years he has terrorised his sister and has been living on her poor earnings."

Gonsalez nodded.

"I saw grey hair in his hands and I guessed what had happened," he said.

"Now what are you going to do?" asked the Earl of Pertham.

Leon was smoking now.

"What are *you* going to do?" he asked in retort. "Perhaps you would like me to tell you?"

"I should," said the man earnestly.

"You are going to take your bigamous wife abroad just as soon as this inquest is over, and you are going to wait a reasonable time and then persuade your wife to get a divorce. After which you will marry your Mrs Prothero in your own name," said Gonsalez.

"Leon," said Manfred after Fearnside had gone back to the room above, the room he had taken in the hope of discovering how much Gonsalez knew, "I think you are a thoroughly unmoral person. Suppose Lady Pertham does not divorce his lordship?"

Leon laughed.

"There is really no need for her to divorce Lord Pertham," he said, "for his lordship told us a little lie. He married his Martha first, deserted her and went back to her. I happen to know this because I have already examined both registers, and I know there was a Mrs Prothero before there was a Lady Pertham."

"You're a wonderful fellow, Leon," said Manfred admiringly.

"I am," admitted Leon Gonsalez.

THE MAN WHO LOVED MUSIC

The most striking characteristics of Mr Homer Lynne were his deep and wide sympathies, and his love of Tschaikovsky's "1812." He loved music generally, but his neighbours in Pennerthon Road, Hampstead, could testify with vehemence and asperity to his preference for that great battle piece. It had led from certain local unpleasantness to a police-court application, having as its object the suppression of Mr Homer Lynne as a public nuisance, and finally to the exchange of lawyers' letters and the threat of an action in the High Court.

That so sympathetic and kindly a gentleman should utterly disregard the feelings and desires of his neighbours, that he should have in his bedroom the largest gramophone that Hampstead had ever known, and a gramophone, moreover, fitted with an automatic arm, so that no sooner was the record finished than the needle was switched to the outer edge of the disc and began all over again, and that he should choose the midnight hour for his indulgence, were facts as strange as they were deplorable.

Mr Lynne had urged at the police court that the only method he had discovered for soothing his nerves that he could ensure himself a night's sleep, was to hear that thunderous piece.

That Mr Lynne was sympathetic at least three distressed parents could testify. He was a theatrical agent with large interests in South America; he specialised in the collection of "turns" for some twenty halls large and small, and the great artists who had travelled through the Argentine and Mexico, Chile and Brazil, had nothing but praise for the excellent treatment they had received at the hands of those

Mr Lynne represented. It was believed, and was, in truth, a fact, that he was financially interested in quite a number of these places of amusement, which may have accounted for the courtesy and attention which the great performers received on their tour.

He also sent out a number of small artists – microscopically small artists whose names had never figured on the play bills of Britain. They were chosen for their beauty, their sprightliness and their absence of ties.

"It's a beautiful country," Mr Homer Lynne would say.

He was a grave, smooth man, clean-shaven, save for a sign of grey side-whiskers, and people who did not know him would imagine that he was a successful lawyer, with an ecclesiastical practice.

"It's a beautiful country," he would say, "but I don't know whether I like sending a young girl to live out there. Of course, you'll have a good salary, and live well – have you any relations?"

If the girl produced a brother or a father, or even a mother, or an intimate maiden aunt, Mr Lynne would nod and promise to write on the morrow, a promise which he fulfilled, regretting that he did not think the applicant would quite suit his purpose – which was true. But if she were isolated from these connections, if there were no relations to whom she would write, or friends who were likely to pester him with enquiries, her first-class passage was forthcoming – but not for the tour which the great artists followed, nor for the bigger halls where they would be likely to meet. They were destined for smaller halls, which were not so much theatre as cabaret.

Now and again, on three separate occasions to be exact, the applicants for an engagement would basely deceive him. She would say she had no relations, and lo! there would appear an inquisitive brother, or, as in the present case, a father.

On a bright morning in June, Mr Lynne sat in his comfortable chair, his hands folded, regarding gravely a nervous little man who sat on the other side of the big mahogany desk balancing his bowler hat on his knees.

"Rosie Goldstein," said Mr Lynne thoughtfully, "I seem to remember the name."

He rang a bell and a dark young man answered.

"Bring me my engagement book, Mr Mandez," said Mr Lynne.

"You see how it is, Mr Lynne," said the caller anxiously – he was unmistakably Hebraic and very nervous. "I hadn't any idea that Rosie had gone abroad until a friend of hers told me that she had come here and got an engagement."

"I see," said Mr Lynne. "She did not tell you she was going."

"No, sir."

The dark young man returned with the book and Mr Lynne turned the pages leisurely, running his finger down a list of names.

"Here we are," he said. "Rosie Goldstein. Yes, I remember the girl now, but she told me she was an orphan."

Goldstein nodded.

"I suppose she thought I'd stop her," he said with a sigh of relief. "But as long as I know where she is, I'm not so worried. Have you her present address?"

Lynne closed the book carefully and beamed at the visitor.

"I haven't her present address," he said cheerfully, "but if you will write her a letter and address it to me, I will see that it goes forward to our agents in Buenos Aires: they, of course, will be able to find her. You see, there are a large number of halls in connection with the circuit, and it is extremely likely that she may be performing up-country. It is quite impossible to keep track of every artist."

"I understand that, sir," said the grateful little Jew.

"She ought to have told you," said the sympathetic Lynne, shaking his head.

He really meant that she ought to have told him.

"However, we'll see what can be done."

He offered his plump hand to the visitor, and the dark young man showed him to the door.

Three minutes later Mr Lynne was interviewing a pretty girl who had the advantage of stage experience – she had been a member of a beauty chorus in a travelling revue. And when the eager girl had answered questions relating to her stage experiences, which were few, Mr Lynne came to the real crux of the interview.

"Now what do your father and mother say about this idea of your accepting this engagement to go abroad?" he asked with his most benevolent smile.

"I have no father or mother," said the girl, and Mr Lynne guessed from the momentary quiver of her lips that she had lost one of these recently.

"You have brothers, perhaps?"

"I have no brothers," she answered, shaking her head. "I haven't any relations in the world, Mr Lynne. You will let me go, won't you?" she pleaded.

Mr Lynne would let her go. If the truth be told, the minor "artists" he sent to the South American continent were infinitely more profitable than the great performers whose names were household words in London.

"I will write you tomorrow," he said conventionally.

"You will let me go?"

He smiled.

"You are certain to go, Miss Hacker. You need have no fear on the subject. I will send you on the contract – no, you had better come here and sign it."

The girl ran down the stairs into Leicester Square, her heart singing. An engagement at three times bigger than the biggest salary she had ever received! She wanted to tell everybody about it, though she did not dream that in a few seconds she would babble her happiness to a man who at that moment was a perfect stranger.

He was a foreign-looking gentleman, well dressed and good-looking. He had the kind of face that appeals to children – an appeal that no psychologist has ever yet analysed.

She met him literally by accident. He was standing at the bottom of the stairs as she came down, and missing her footing she fell forward into his arms.

"I am ever so sorry," she said with a smile.

"You don't look very sorry," smiled the man. "You look more like a person who had just got a very nice engagement to go abroad."

She stared at him.

"However did you know that?"

"I know it because – well, I know," he laughed, and apparently abandoning his intention of going upstairs, he turned and walked with her into the street.

"Yes, I am," she nodded. "I've had a wonderful opportunity. Are you in the profession?"

"No, I'm not in the profession," said Leon Gonsalez, "if you mean the theatrical profession, but I know the countries you're going to rather well. Would you like to hear something about the Argentine?"

She looked at him dubiously.

"I should very much," she hesitated, "but I – "

"I'm going to have a cup of tea, come along," said Leon good-humouredly.

Though she had no desire for tea or even for the interview (though she was dying to tell somebody) the magnetic personality of the man held her, and she fell in by his side. And at that very moment Mr Lynne was saying to the dark-skinned man:

"Fonso! She's a beaut!" and that staid man kissed the bunched tips of his fingers ecstatically.

This was the third time Leon Gonsalez had visited the elegant offices of Mr Homer Lynne in Panton Street.

Once there was an organisation which was called the Four Just Men, and these had banded themselves together to execute justice upon those whom the law had missed, or passed by, and had earned for themselves a reputation which was world-wide. One had died, and of the three who were left, Poiccart (who had been called the brains of the four) was living quietly in Seville. To him had come a letter from a compatriot in Rio, a compatriot who did not identify him with the organisation of the Four Just Men, but had written vehemently of certain abominations. There had been an exchange of letters, and Poiccart had discovered that most of these fresh English girls who had appeared in the dance halls of obscure towns had been imported through the agency of the respectable Mr Lynne, and Poiccart had written to his friends in London.

"Yes, it's a beautiful country," said Leon Gonsalez, stirring his tea thoughtfully. "I suppose you're awfully pleased with yourself."

"Oh, it's wonderful," said the girl. "Fancy, I'm going to receive £12 a week and my board and lodging. Why, I shall be able to save almost all of it."

"Have you any idea where you will perform?"

The girl smiled.

"I don't know the country," she said, "and it's dreadfully ignorant of me, but I don't know one single town in the Argentine."

"There aren't many people who do," smiled Leon, "but you've heard of Brazil, I suppose?"

"Yes, it's a little country in South America," she nodded, "I know that."

"Where the nuts come from," laughed Leon. "No, it's not a little country in South America: it's a country as wide as from here to the centre of Persia, and as long as Brighton to the equator. Does that give you any idea?"

She stared at him.

And then he went on, but confined himself to the physical features of the sub-continent. Not once did he refer to her contract – that was not his object. That object was disclosed, though not to her, when he said:

"I must send you a book, Miss Hacker: it will interest you if you are going to the Argentine. It is full of very accurate information."

"Oh, thank you," she said gratefully. "Shall I give you my address?"

That was exactly what Leon had been fishing for. He put the scrap of paper she had written on into his pocket-book, and left her.

George Manfred, who had acquired a two-seater car, picked him up outside the National Gallery, and drove him to Kensington Gardens, the refreshment buffet of which, at this hour of the day, was idle. At one of the deserted tables Leon disclosed the result of his visit.

"It was singularly fortunate that I should have met one of the lambs."

"Did you see Lynne himself?"

Leon nodded.

"After I left the girl I went up and made a call. It was rather difficult to get past the Mexican gentleman – Mandez I think his name is – into the sanctum but eventually Lynne saw me."

He chuckled softly:

"I do not play on the banjo; I declare this to you, my dear George, in all earnestness. The banjo to me is a terrible instrument – "

"Which means," said Manfred with a smile, "that you described yourself as a banjo soloist who wanted a job in South America."

"Exactly," said Leon, "and I need hardly tell you that I was not engaged. The man is interesting, George."

"All men are interesting to you, Leon," laughed Manfred, putting aside the coffee he had ordered, and lighting a long, thin cigar.

"I should have loved to tell him that his true vocation was arson. He has the face of the true incendiary, and I tell you George, that Lombroso was never more accurate than when he described that type. A fair, clear, delicate skin, a plump, baby like face, hair extraordinarily fine: you can pick them out anywhere."

He caressed his chin and frowned.

"Callous destruction of human happiness also for profit. I suppose the same type of mind would commit both crimes. It is an interesting parallel. I should like to consult our dear friend Poiccart on that subject."

"Can he be touched by the law?" asked Manfred. "Is there no way of betraying him?"

"Absolutely none," said Leon shortly. "The man is a genuine agent. He has the names of some of the best people on his books and they all speak loudly in his praise. The lie that is half a lie is easier to detect than the criminal who is half honest. If the chief cashier of the Bank of England turned forger, he would be the most successful forger in the world. This man has covered himself at every point. I had a talk with a Jewish gentleman – a pathetic old soul named Goldstein, whose daughter went abroad some seven or eight months ago. He has not heard from her, and he told me that Lynne was very surprised to discover that she had any relations at all. The unrelated girl is his best investment."

"Did Lynne give the old man her address?"

Leon shrugged his shoulders.

"There are a million square miles in the Argentine – where is she? Cordoba, Tucuman, Mendoza, San Louis, Santa Fé, Rio Cuarto, those are a few towns. And there are hundreds of towns where this girl may be dancing, towns which have no British or American Consul. It's rather horrible, George."

Manfred looked thoughtfully across the green spaces in the park.

"If we could be sure," said Gonsalez softly. "It will take exactly two months to satisfy us, and I think it would be worth the money. Our young friend will leave by the next South American packet, and you, some time ago, were thinking of returning to Spain. I think I will take the trip."

George nodded.

"I thought you would," he said. "I really can't see how we can act unless you do."

Miss Lilah Hacker was amazed when she boarded the *Braganza* at Boulogne to discover that she had as fellow passenger the polite stranger who had lectured so entertainingly on the geography of South America.

To the girl her prospect was rosy and bright. She was looking forward to a land of promise, her hopes for the future were at zenith, and if she was disappointed a little that the agreeable Gonsalez did not keep her company on the voyage, but seemed for ever preoccupied, that was a very unimportant matter.

It was exactly a month from the day she put foot on the *Braganza* that her hope and not a little of her faith in humanity were blasted by a stout Irishman whose name was Rafferty, but who had been born in the Argentine. He was the proprietor of a dance hall called "La Plaza" in a cattle town in the interior. She had been sent there with two other girls wiser than she, to entertain the half-breed vaqueros who thronged the town at night, and for whom "La Plaza" was the principal attraction.

"You've got to get out of them ways of yours," said Rafferty, twisting his cigar from one side of his mouth to the other. "When

Senor Santiago wanted you to sit on his knee last night, you made a fuss, I'm told."

"Of course, I did," said the girl indignantly. "Why, he's coloured!"

"Now see here," said Mr Rafferty, "there ain't no coloured people in this country. Do you get that? Mr Santiago is a gentleman and he's got stacks of money, and the next time he pays you a little attention, you've got to be pleasant, see?"

"I'll do nothing of the sort," said the girl, pale and shaking, "and I'm going straight back to Buenos Aires tonight."

"Oh you are, are you?" Rafferty smiled broadly. "That's an idea you can get out of your head, too."

Suddenly he gripped her by the arm.

"You're going up to your room, now," he said, "and you're going to stay there till I bring you out tonight to do your show, and if you give me any of your nonsense – you'll be sorry!"

He pushed her through the rough unpainted door of the little cell which was termed bedroom, and he paused in the doorway to convey information (and there was a threat in the course of it) which left her white and staring.

She came down that night and did her performance and to her surprise and relief did not excite even the notice of the wealthy Mr Santiago, a half-bred Spaniard with a yellow face, who did not so much as look at her.

Mr Rafferty was also unusually bland and polite.

She went to her room that night feeling more comfortable. Then she discovered that her key was gone, and she sat up until one o'clock in the morning waiting for she knew not what. At that hour came a soft footfall in the passage: somebody tried the handle of her door, but she had braced a chair under the handle. They pushed and the rickety chair creaked; then there was a sound like a stick striking a cushion, and she thought she heard somebody sliding against the wooden outer wall of the room. A tap came to her door.

"Miss Hacker," the voice said. She recognised it immediately. "Open the door quickly. I want to get you away."

With a trembling hand she removed the chair, and the few little articles of furniture she had piled against the door, and opened it. By the light of the candle which was burning in her room she recognised the man who had been her fellow passenger on the *Braganza*.

"Come quietly," he said. "There is a back stair to the compound. Have you a cloak? Bring it, because you have a sixty-mile motor journey before we come to the railway…"

As she came through the door she saw the upturned toes of somebody who was lying in the passage, and with a shudder she realised that was the thumping sound she had heard.

They reached the big yard behind the "Plaza" crowded with the dusty motor cars of ranchers and their foremen, who had come into town for the evening, and passed out through the doorway. A big car was standing in the middle of the road, and to this he guided her. She threw one glance back at Rafferty's bar. The windows blazed with light, the sound of the orchestra came faintly through the still night air, then she dropped her head on her hands and wept.

Leon Gonsalez had a momentary pang of contrition, for he might have saved her all of this.

It was two months exactly from the day he had left London, when he came running up the stairs of the Jermyn Street flat and burst in upon Manfred.

"You're looking fit and fine, Leon," said George, jumping up and gripping his hand. "You didn't write and I never expected that you would. I only got back from Spain two days ago."

He gave the news from Seville, and then:

"You proved the case?"

"To our satisfaction," said Leon grimly. "Though you would not satisfy the law that Lynne was guilty. It is, however, a perfectly clear case. I visited his agent when I was in Buenos Aires, and took the liberty of rifling his desk in his absence. I found several letters from Lynne and by their tone there can be no doubt whatever that Lynne is consciously engaged in this traffic."

They looked at one another.

"The rest is simple," said Manfred, "and I will leave you to work out the details, my dear Leon, with every confidence that Mr Homer Lynne will be very sorry indeed that he departed from the safe and narrow way."

There was no more painstaking, thorough or conscientious workman than Leon Gonsalez. The creation of punishment was to him a work of love. No General ever designed the battle with a more punctilious regard to the minutest detail than Leon.

Before the day was over he had combed the neighbourhood in which Mr Lynne lived of every vital fact. It was then that he learnt of Mr Lynne's passion for music. The cab which took Leon back to Jermyn Street did not go fast enough: he literally leap into the sitting-room, chortling his joy.

"The impossible is possible, my dear George," he cried, pacing about the apartment like a man demented. "I thought I should never be able to carry my scheme into effect, but he loves music, George! He adores the tuneful phonograph!"

"A little ice water, I think," suggested Manfred gently.

"No, no," said Leon, "I am not hot, I am cool: I am ice itself! And who would expect such good luck? Tonight we will drive to Hampstead and we will hear his concert."

It was a long time before he gave a coherent account of what he had learnt. Mr Lynne was extremely unpopular in the neighbourhood, and Leon explained why.

Manfred understood better that night, when the silence of the sedate road in which Mr Lynne's detached house was situated was broken by the shrill sound of trumpets, and the rolling of drums, the clanging of bells, the simulated boom of cannon – all the barbarian musical interjection which has made "1812" so popular with unmusical people.

"It sounds like a real band," said Manfred in surprise.

A policeman strolled along, and seeing the car standing before the house, turned his head with a laugh.

"It's an awful row, isn't it?"

"I wonder it doesn't wake everybody up," suggested Manfred.

"It does," replied the policeman, "or it did until they got used to it. It's the loudest gramophone in the world, I should think: like one of those things you have at the bottom of the tube stairs, to tell the people to move on. A stentaphone, isn't it?"

"How long does this go on? All night?" asked Manfred.

"For about an hour, I believe," said the policeman. "The gentleman who lives in that house can't go to sleep without music. He's a bit artistic, I think."

"He is," said Leon grimly.

The next day he found out that four servants were kept in the establishment, three of whom slept on the premises. Mr Lynne was in the habit of returning home every evening at about ten o'clock, except on Fridays when he went out of Town.

Wednesday evening was the cook's night out, and it was also the night when Mr Lynne's butler and general factotum was allowed an evening off. There remained the housemaid, and even she presented no difficulty. The real trouble was that all these people would return to the house or the neighbourhood at eleven o'clock. Leon decided to make his appointment with Mr Lynne for Friday night, on which day he usually went to Brighton. He watched the genial man leave Victoria, and then he called up Lynne's house.

"Is that Masters?" he asked, and a man's voice answered him.

"Yes, sir," was the reply.

"It is Mr Mandez here," said Leon, imitating the curious broken English of Lynne's Mexican assistant. "Mr Lynne is returning to the house tonight on very important business, and he does not want any of the servants to be there."

"Indeed, sir," said Masters and showed no surprise. Evidently these instructions had been given before. Leon had expected some difficulty here, and had prepared a very elaborate explanation which it was not necessary to give.

"He wouldn't like me to stay, sir?"

"Oh, no," said Leon. "Mr Lynne particularly said that nobody was to be in the house. He wants the side door and the kitchen door left unlocked," he added as an afterthought. It was a brilliant afterthought if it came off, and apparently it did.

"Very good, sir," said Masters.

Leon went straight from the telephone call-box, where he had sent the message, to the counter and wrote out a wire, addressed to Lynne, Hotel Ritz, Brighton. The message ran:

"The girl Goldstein has been discovered at Santa Fé. Terrible row. Police have been making enquiries. Have very important information for you. I am waiting for you at your house."

He signed it Mandez.

"He will get the wire at eight. There is a train back at nine. That should bring him to Hampstead by half past ten," said Leon when he had rejoined Manfred who was waiting for him outside the post office.

"We will be there an hour earlier: that is as soon as it is dark."

They entered the house without the slightest difficulty. Manfred left his two-seater outside a doctor's house, a place where an unattended car would not be noticed, and went on foot to Lynne's residence. It was a large detached house, expensively furnished, and as Leon had expected, the servants had gone. He located Lynne's room, a big apartment at the front of the house.

"There is his noise box," said Leon, pointing to a handsome cabinet near the window. "Electrical, too. Where does that wire lead?"

He followed the flex to a point above the head of the bed, where it terminated in what looked like a hanging bell push.

Leon was momentarily puzzled and then a light dawned upon him.

"Of course, if he has this infernal noise to make him go to sleep, the bell push switches off the music and saves him getting out of bed."

He opened the lid of the gramophone cabinet and examined the record.

"1812," he chuckled. He lifted the needle from the disc, turned the switch and the green table revolved. Then he walked to the head of the bed and pushed the knob of the bell push. Instantly the revolutions stopped.

"That is it," he nodded, and turned over the soundbox, letting the needle rest upon the edge of the record.

"That," he pointed to a bronze rod which ran from the centre of the side of the disc and fitted to some adjustment in the soundbox, "is the repeater. It is an American invention which I saw in Buenos Aires, but I haven't seen many on this side. When the record is finished the rod automatically transfers the needle to the beginning of the record."

"So that it can go on and on and on," said Manfred interested. "I don't wonder our friend is unpopular."

Leon was looking round the room for something and at last he found what he was seeking. It was a brass clothes peg fastened to a door which led to a dressing-room. He put all his weight on the peg but it held firm.

"Excellent," he said, and opened his bag. From this he took a length of stout cord and skilfully knotted one end to the clothes hook. He tested it but it did not move. From the bag he took a pair of handcuffs, unlocked and opened them and laid them on the bed. Then he took out what looked to be a Field-Marshal's baton. It was about fourteen inches long, and fastened around were two broad strips of felt; tied neatly to the baton were nine pieces of cord which were fastened at one end to the cylinder. The cords were twice the length of the handle and were doubled over neatly and temporarily fastened to the handle by pieces of twine.

Leon looked at one end of the baton and Manfred saw a red seal.

"What on earth is that, Leon?"

Leon showed him the seal, and Manfred read:

"Prison Commission."

"That," said Leon, "is what is colloquially known as the 'cat'. In other words, the 'cat of nine tails'. It is an authentic instrument which I secured with some difficulty."

He cut the twine that held the cords to the handle and let the nine thongs fall straight. Manfred took them into his hands and examined them curiously. The cords were a little thinner than ordinary window line, but more closely woven: at the end of each thong there was a binding of yellow silk for about half an inch.

Leon took the weapon in his hands and sent the cords whistling round his head.

"Made in Pentonville Gaol," he explained, "and I'm afraid I'm not as expert as the gentleman who usually wields it."

The dusk grew to darkness. The two men made their way downstairs and waited in the room leading from the hall.

At half past ten exactly they heard a key turn in the lock and the door close.

"Are you there, Mandez?" called the voice of Mr Lynne, and it sounded anxious.

He took three steps towards the door and then Gonsalez stepped out.

"Good evening, Mr Lynne," he said.

The man switched on the light.

He saw before him a figure plainly dressed, but who it was he could not guess, for the intruder's face was covered by a white semi-diaphanous veil.

"Who are you? What do you want?" gasped Lynne.

"I want you," said Leon shortly. "Before we go any further, I will tell you this, Mr Lynne, that if you make an outcry, if you attempt to attract attention from outside, it will be the last sound you ever make."

"What do you want of me?" asked the stout man shakily, and then his eyes fell upon Manfred similarly veiled and he collapsed into the hall chair.

Manfred gripped his arm and led him upstairs to his bedroom. The blinds were pulled and the only light came from a small table-lamp by the side of the bed.

"Take off your coat," said Manfred.

Mr Lynne obeyed.

"Now your waistcoat."

The waistcoat was discarded.

"Now I fear I shall have to have your shirt," said Gonsalez.

"What are you going to do?" asked the man hoarsely.

"I will tell you later."

The stout man, his face twitching, stood bare to the waist, and offered no resistance when Manfred snapped the handcuffs on him.

They led him to the door where the hat peg was and deftly Leon slipped the loose ends of the rope through the links and pulled his manacled hands tightly upwards.

"Now we can talk," said Gonsalez. "Mr Lynne, for some time you have been engaged in abominable traffic. You have been sending women, who sometimes were no more than children, to South America, and the penalties for that crime are, as you know, a term of imprisonment and this."

He picked the baton from where he had opened it, and shook out the loose cords. Mr Lynne gazed at them over his shoulder, with a fascinated stare.

"This is colloquially known as the 'cat of nine tails'," said Gonsalez, and sent the thongs shrilling round his head.

"I swear to you I never knew – " blubbered the man. "You can't prove it – "

"I do not intend proving it in public," said Leon carefully. "I am here merely to furnish proof to you that you cannot break the law and escape punishment."

And then it was that Manfred started the gramophone revolving, and the blare of trumpets and the thunder of drums filled the room with strident harmony.

The same policeman to whom Manfred and Gonsalez had spoken a few nights previously paced slowly past the house and stopped to listen with a grin. So, too, did a neighbour.

"What a din that thing makes," said the aggrieved householder.

"Yes it does," admitted the policeman. "I think he wants a new record. It sounds almost as though somebody was shrieking their head off, doesn't it?"

"It always sounds like that to me," grumbled the neighbour, and went on.

The policeman smiled and resumed his beat, and from behind the windows of Mr Lynne's bedroom came the thrilling cadences of the "Marseillaise" and the boom of guns, and a shrill thin sound of fear and pain for which Tschaikovsky was certainly not responsible.

THE MAN WHO WAS PLUCKED

On Sunday night Martaus Club is always crowded with the smartest of the smart people who remain in Town over the weekend. Martaus Club is a place of shaded lights, of white napery, of glittering silver and glass, of exotic flowers, the tables set about the walls framing a parallelogram of shining floor.

Young men and women, and older folks too, can be very happy in Martaus Club – at a price. It is not the size of the "note" which Louis, the head waiter, initials, nor the amazing cost of wine, nor the half-a-crown strawberries, that breaks a man.

John Eden could have footed the bill for all he ate or drank or smoked in Martaus, and in truth the club was as innocent as it was gay. A pack of cards had never been found within its portals. Louis knew every face and the history behind the face, and could have told within a few pounds just what was the bank balance of every habitué. He did not know John Eden, who was the newest of members, but he guessed shrewdly.

John Eden had danced with a strange girl, which was unusual at Martaus, for you bring your own dancing partner, and never under any circumstances solicit a dance with a stranger.

But Welby was there. Jack knew him slightly, though he had not seen him for years. Welby was the mirror of fashion and apparently a person of some importance. When he came across to him, Jack felt rather like a country cousin. He had been eight years in South Africa, and he felt rather out of it, but Welby was kindness itself, and then and there insisted upon introducing him to Maggie Vane. A beautiful girl, beautifully gowned, magnificently jewelled – her pearl necklace cost £20,000 – she rather took poor Jack's breath away, and when she suggested that they should go to Bingley's, he would not have dreamt of refusing.

As he passed out through the lobby Louis, the head waiter, with an apology, brushed a little bit of fluff from his dress-coat, and said in a voice, inaudible, save to Jack:

"Don't go to Bingley's," which was of course a preposterous piece of impertinence, and Jack glared at him.

He was at Bingley's until six o'clock in the morning, and left behind him cheques which would absorb every penny he had brought back from Africa, and a little more. He had come home dreaming of a little estate with a little shooting and a little fishing, and the writing of that book of his on big-game hunting, and all his dreams went out when the croupier, with a smile on his bearded lips, turned a card with a mechanical:

"*Le Rouge gagnant et couleur.*"

He had never dreamt Bingley's was a gambling-house, and it certainly had not that appearance when he went in. It was only when this divine girl introduced him to the inner room, where they played *trente-et-quarante* and he saw how high the stakes were running, that he began to feel nervous. He sat by her side at the table and staked modestly and won. And continued to win – until he increased his stakes.

They were very obliging at Bingley's. They accepted cheques, and, indeed, had cheque forms ready to be filled in.

Jack Eden came back to the flat he had taken in Jermyn Street, which was immediately above that occupied by Manfred and Leon Gonsalez, and wrote a letter to his brother in India…

Manfred heard the shot and woke up. He came out into the sitting-room in his pyjamas to find Leon already there looking at the ceiling, the whitewash of which was discoloured by a tiny red patch which was growing larger.

Manfred went out on to the landing and found the proprietor of the flats in his shirt and trousers, for he had heard the shot from his basement apartment.

"I thought it was in your room, sir," he said, "it must be in Mr Eden's apartment."

Going up the stairs he explained that Mr Eden was a new arrival in the country. The door of his flat was locked, but the proprietor produced a key which opened it. The lights were burning in the sitting-room, and one glance told Manfred the whole story. A huddled figure was lying across the table, from which the blood was dripping and forming a pool on the floor.

Gonsalez handled the man scientifically.

"He is not dead," he said. "I doubt if the bullet has touched any vital organ."

The man had shot himself in the breast; from the direction of the wound Gonsalez was fairly sure that the injuries were minor. He applied a first-aid dressing and together they lifted him on to a sofa. Then when the wound was dressed, Gonsalez looked round and saw the tell-tale letter.

"Pinner," he said, holding the letter up, "I take it that you do not want to advertise the fact that somebody attempted to commit suicide in one of your flats?"

"That is the last thing in the world I want," said the flat proprietor, fervently.

"Then I'm going to put this letter in my pocket. Will you telephone to the hospital to say there has been an accident. Don't talk about suicide. The gentleman has recently come back from South Africa; he was packing his pistol, and it exploded."

The man nodded and left the room hurriedly.

Gonsalez went to where Eden was lying and it was at that moment the young man's eyes opened. He looked from Manfred to Gonsalez with a puzzled frown.

"My friend," said Leon, in a gentle voice as he leant over the wounded man, "you have had an accident, you understand? You are not fatally injured; in fact, I think your injury is a very slight one. The ambulance will come for you and you will go to a hospital and I will visit you daily."

"Who are you?" whispered the man.

"I am a neighbour of yours," smiled Leon.

"The letter!" Eden gasped the words and Leon nodded.

"I have it in my pocket," he said, "and I will restore it to you when you are recovered. You understand that you have had an accident?"

Eden nodded.

A quarter of an hour later the hospital ambulance rolled up to the door, and the would-be suicide was taken away.

"Now," said Leon, when they were back in their own room, "we will discover what all this is about," and very calmly he slit open the envelope and read.

"What is it?" asked Manfred.

"Our young friend came back from South Africa with £7,000, which he had accumulated in eight years of hard work. He lost it in less than eight hours at a gambling-house which he does not specify. He has not only lost all the money he has but more, and apparently has given cheques to meet his debts."

Leon scratched his chin.

"That necessitates a further examination of his room. I wonder if the admirable Mr Pinner will object?"

The admirable Mr Pinner was quite willing that Leon should anticipate the inevitable visit of the police. The search was made, and Leon found a cheque-book for which he had been looking, tucked away in the inside pocket of Jack Eden's dress-suit and brought it down to his room.

"No names," he said disappointedly. "Just 'cash' on every counterfoil. All, I should imagine, to the same person. He banks with the Third National Bank of South Africa, which has an office in Throgmorton Street."

He carefully copied the numbers of the cheques – there were ten in all.

"First of all," he said, "as soon as the post office is open we will send a telegram to the bank stopping the payment of these. Of course he

113

can be sued, but a gambling debt is not recoverable at law, and before that happens we shall see many developments."

The first development came the next afternoon. Leon had given instructions that anybody who called for Mr Eden was to be shown up to him, and at three o'clock came a very smartly dressed young man who aspirated his h's with suspicious emphasis.

"Is this Mr Eden's flat?"

"No, it isn't," said Gonsalez. "It is the flat of myself and my friend who are acting for Mr Eden."

The visitor frowned suspiciously at Leon.

"Acting for him?" he said. "Well, you can perhaps give me a little information about some cheques that have been stopped. My governor went to get a special clearance this morning, and the bank refused payment. Does Mr Eden know all about this?"

"Who is your governor?" asked Leon pleasantly.

"Mr Mortimer Birn."

"And his address?"

The young man gave it. Mr Mortimer Birn was apparently a bill-discounter, and had cashed the cheques for a number of people who did not want to pass them through their banks. The young man was very emphatic as to the cheques being the property of a large number of people.

"And they all came to Mr Birn. What a singular coincidence," agreed Leon.

"I'd rather see Mr Eden, if you don't mind," said the emissary of Mr Mortimer Birn, and his tone was unpleasant.

"You cannot see him because he has met with an accident," said Leon. "But I will see your Mr Birn."

He found Mr Birn in a very tiny office in Glasshouse Street. The gentleman's business was not specified either on the door-plate or on the painted window, but Leon smelt "money-lender" the moment he went into his office.

The outer office was unoccupied when he entered. It was a tiny dusty cupboard of a place with just room enough to put a diminutive table, and the space was further curtailed by a wooden partition, head high, which served to exclude the unfortunate person who occupied the room from draughts and immediate observation. A door marked private led to Mr Birn's holy of holies and from this room came the sound of loud voices.

Gonsalez listened.

"...come without telephoning, hey? She always comes in the morning, haven't I told you a hundred times?" roared one voice.

"She doesn't know me," grumbled the other.

"She's only got to see your hair..."

It was at that moment that the young man who called at Jermyn Street came out of the room. Gonsalez had a momentary glimpse of two men. One was short and stout, the other was tall, but it was his bright red hair that caught Leon's eye. And then Mr Birn's clerk went back to the room and the voices ceased. When Gonsalez was ushered into the office, only the proprietor of the establishment was visible.

Birn was a stout bald man, immensely affable. He told Leon the same story as his clerk had told.

"Now, what is Eden going to do about these cheques?" asked Birn at last.

"I don't think he's going to meet them," said Leon gently. "You see, they are gambling debts."

"They are cheques," interrupted Birn, "and a cheque is a cheque whether it's for a gambling debt or a sack of potatoes."

"Is that the law?" asked Leon, "and if it is, will you write me a letter to that effect, in which case you will be paid."

"Certainly I will," said Mr Birn. "If that's all you want, I'll write it now."

"Proceed," said Leon, but Mr Birn did not write the letter.

Instead he talked about his lawyers; grew virtuously indignant on the unsportsmanlike character of people who repudiated debts of honour (how he came to be satisfied that the cheques represented gambling losses, he did not explain) and ended the interview a little apoplectically. And all the time Leon was speculating upon the identity of the third man he had seen and who had evidently left the room through one of the three doors which opened from the office.

Leon went down the narrow stairs into the street, and as he stepped on to the pavement, a little car drove up and a girl descended. She did not look at him, but brushing past ran up the stairs. She was alone, and had driven her own luxurious coupé. Gonsalez, who was interested, waited till she came out, which was not for twenty minutes, and she was obviously distressed.

Leon was curious and interested. He went straight on to the hospital where they had taken Eden, and found the young man sufficiently recovered to be able to talk.

His first words betrayed his anxiety and his contrition.

"I say, what did you do with that letter? I was a fool to – "

"Destroyed it," said Leon, which was true. "Now, my young friend, you've got to tell me something. Where was the gambling-house to which you went?"

It took a long time to persuade Mr John Eden that he was not betraying a confidence and then he told him the whole story from beginning to end.

"So it was a lady who took you there, eh?" said Leon thoughtfully.

"She wasn't in it," said John Eden quickly. "She was just a visitor like myself. She told me she had lost five hundred pounds."

"Naturally, naturally," said Leon. "Is she a fair lady with very blue eyes, and has she a little car of her own?"

The man looked surprised.

"Yes, she drove me in her car," he said, "and she is certainly fair and has blue eyes. In fact, she's one of the prettiest girls I've ever seen. You needn't worry about the lady, sir," he said shaking his head. "Poor girl, she was victimised, if there was any victimisation."

"196 Paul Street, Mayfair, I think you said."

"I'm certain it was Paul Street, and almost as sure it was 196," said Eden. "But I hope you're not going to take any action against them, because it was my own fault. Aren't you one of the two gentlemen who live in the flat under me?" he asked suddenly.

Leon nodded.

"I suppose the cheques have been presented and some of them have come back."

"They have not been presented yet, or at any rate they have not been honoured," said Leon. "And had you shot yourself, my young friend, they would not have been honoured at all, because your bank would have stopped payment automatically."

Manfred dined alone that night. Leon had not returned, and there had been no news from him until eight o'clock, when there came a District Messenger with a note asking Manfred to give the bearer his dress clothes and one or two articles which he mentioned.

Manfred was too used to the ways of Leon Gonsalez to be greatly surprised. He packed a small suitcase, sent the messenger boy off with it and he himself spent the evening writing letters.

At half past two he heard a slight scuffle in the street outside, and Leon came in without haste, and in no wise perturbed, although he had just emerged from a rough-and-tumble encounter with a young man who had been watching the house all the evening for his return.

He was not in evening dress, Manfred noticed, but was wearing the clothes he had on when he went out in the morning.

"You got your suitcase all right?"

"Oh yes, quite," replied Leon.

He took a short stick from his trousers pocket, a stick made of rhinoceros hide, and called in South Africa a "sjambok". It was about a foot and a half in length, but it was a formidable weapon and was one of the articles which Leon had asked for. He examined it in the light.

"No, I didn't cut his scalp," he said. "I was afraid I had."

"Who was this?"

Before he replied, Leon put out the light, pulled back the curtains from the open window and looked out. He came back, replaced the curtains, and put the light on again.

"He has gone away, but I do not think we have seen the last of that crowd," he said.

He drank a glass of water, sat down by the table and laughed.

"Do you realise, my dear Manfred," he said, "that we have a friend in Mr Fare, the Police Commissioner, and that he occasionally visits us?"

"I realise that very well," smiled Manfred. "Why, have you seen him?"

Leon shook his head.

"No, only other people have seen him and have associated me with the Metropolitan Constabulary. I had occasion to interview our friend Mr Bingley, and he and those who are working with him are perfectly satisfied that I am what is known in London as a 'split', in other words a detective, and it is generally believed that I am engaged in the business of suppressing gambling-houses. Hence the mild attention I have received and hence the fact, as I recognised when I was on my way back to Jermyn Street today – luckily I had forgotten to tell the cabman where to stop and he passed the watchers before I could stop him – that I am under observation."

He described his visit to the hospital and his interview with Mr Birn.

"Birn, who of course is Bingley, is the proprietor of three, and probably more, big gambling-houses in London, at least he is the financial power behind them. I should not imagine that he himself frequents any of them. The house in Mayfair was, of course, shut up tonight and I did not attempt to locate it. They were afraid that our poor friend would inform the police. But oh, my dear Manfred, how can I describe to you the beauties of that lovely house in Bayswater Road, where all that is fashionable and wealthy in London gathers every night to try its luck at baccarat?"

"How did you get there?" asked Manfred.

"I was taken," replied Gonsalez simply. "I went to dinner at Martaus Club. I recognised Mr Welby and greeted him as an old friend. I think he really believed that he had met me before I went to the Argentine and made my pile, and of course, he sat down with me and we drank liqueurs, and he introduced me to a most beautiful girl, with a most perfectly upholstered little run-about."

"You weren't recognised?"

Leon shook his head.

"The moustache which I put on my face was indistinguishable from the real thing," he said not without pride. "I put it on hair by hair, and it took me two hours to manufacture. When it was done you would not have recognised me. I danced with the beautiful Margaret and – " he hesitated.

"You made love to her," said Manfred admiringly.

Leon shrugged.

"My dear Manfred, it was necessary," he said solemnly. "And was it not fortunate that I had in my pocket a diamond ring which I had brought back from South America – it cost me 110 guineas in Regent Street this afternoon – and how wonderful that it should fit her. She wasn't feeling at her best, either, until that happened. That was the price of my admission to the Bayswater establishment. She drove me there in her car. It was a visit not without profit," he said modestly. He put his hand in his pocket and pulled out a stiff bundle of notes.

Manfred was laughing softly.

Leon was the cleverest manipulator of cards in Europe. His long delicate fingers, the amazing rapidity with which he could move them, his natural gift for palming, would have made his fortune either as a conjurer or a card-sharper.

"The game was baccarat and the cards were dealt from a box by an intelligent croupier," explained Leon. "Those which were used were thrown into a basin. Those in the stack were, of course, so carefully arranged that the croupier knew the sequence of them all. To secure a dozen cards from the basin was a fairly simple matter. To stroll from the room and rearrange them so that they were alternately against and for the bank, was not difficult, but to place them on the top of those he was dealing, my dear Manfred, I was an artist!"

Leon did not explain what form his artistry took, nor how he directed the attention of croupier and company away from the "deck" for that fraction of a second necessary – the croupier seldom took his hands from the cards – but the results of his enterprise were to be found in the thick stack of notes which lay on the table.

He took off his coat and put on his old velvet jacket, pacing the room with his hands in his pockets.

"Margaret Vane," he said softly. "One of God's most beautiful works, George, flawless, gifted, and yet if she is what she appears, something so absolutely loathsome that…"

He shook his head sadly.

"Does she play a big part, or is she just a dupe?" asked Manfred.

Leon did not answer at once.

"I'm rather puzzled," he said slowly. He related his experience in Mr Birn's office, the glimpse of the red-haired man and Mr Birn's fury with him.

"I do not doubt that the 'she' to whom reference was made was Margaret Vane. But that alone would not have shaken my faith in her guilt. After I left the Bayswater house I decided that I would discover where she was living. She had so skilfully evaded any question on this matter which I had put to her that I grew suspicious. I hired a taxicab and waited, sitting inside. Presently her car came out and I followed her. Mr Birn had a house in Fitzroy Square and it was to there she drove. A man was waiting outside to take her car, and she went straight into the house, letting herself in. It was at this point that I began to think that Birn and she were much better friends than I had thought.

"I decided to wait, and stopped the car on the other side of the Square. In about a quarter of an hour the girl came out, and to my surprise, she had changed her clothes. I dismissed the cab and followed on foot. She lives at 803 Gower Street."

"That certainly is puzzling," agreed Manfred. "The thing does not seem to dovetail, Leon."

"That is what I think," nodded Leon. "I am going to 803 Gower Street tomorrow morning."

Gonsalez required very little sleep and ten o'clock in the morning was afoot.

The report he brought back to Manfred was interesting.

"Her name is Elsie Chaucer, and she lives with her father, who is paralysed in both legs. They have a flat, one servant and a nurse, whose business it is to attend to the father. Nothing is known of them except that they have seen better times. The father spends the day with a pack of cards, working out a gambling system, and probably that explains their poverty. He is never seen by visitors, and the girl is supposed to be an actress – that is supposed by the landlady. It is rather queer," said Gonsalez thoughtfully. "The solution is, of course, in Birn's house and in Birn's mind."

"I think we will get at that, Leon."

Leon nodded.

"So I thought," said he. "Mr Birn's establishment does not present any insuperable difficulties."

Mr Birn was at home that night. He was at home most nights. Curled up in a deep armchair, he puffed at a long and expensive cigar, and read the *London Gazette* which was to him the most interesting piece of literature which the genius of Caxton had made possible.

At midnight his housekeeper came in. She was a middle-aged Frenchwoman and discreet.

"All right?" queried Mr Birn lazily.

"No, monsieur, I desire that you speak to Charles."

Charles was Mr Birn's chauffeur, and between Charles and Madame was a continuous feud.

"What has Charles been doing?" asked Mr Birn with a frown.

"He is admitted every evening to the kitchen for supper," explained madame, "and it is an order that he should close the door after he goes out. But, m'sieur, when I went this evening at eleven o'clock to bolt the door, it was not closed. If I had not put on the lights and with my own eyes have seen it, the door would have been open, and we might have been murdered in our beds."

"I'll talk to him in the morning," growled Mr Birn. "You've left the door of mademoiselle's room unfastened?"

"Yes, m'sieur, the key is in the lock."

"Good night," said Mr Birn resuming his study. At half past two he heard the street door close gently and a light footstep passed through the hall. He looked up at the clock, threw away the end of his cigar and lit another before he rose and went heavily to a wall safe. This he unlocked and took out an empty steel box, which he opened and placed on the table. Then he resumed his chair.

Presently came a light tap at the door.

"Come in," said Mr Birn.

The girl who was variously called Vane and Chaucer came into the room. She was neatly but not richly dressed. In many ways the plainness of her street costume enhanced her singular beauty and Mr Birn gazed approvingly upon her refreshing figure.

"Sit down, Miss Chaucer," he said, putting out his hand for the little linen bag she carried.

He opened it and took out a rope of pearls and examined every gem separately.

"I haven't stolen any," she said contemptuously.

"Perhaps you haven't," said Mr Birn, "but I've known some funny things happen."

He took the diamond pin, the rings, the two diamond and emerald bracelets, and each of these he scrutinised before he returned them to the bag and put the bag into the steel box.

He did not speak until he had placed them in the safe.

"Well, how are things going tonight?" he asked.

She shrugged her shoulders.

"I take no interest in gambling," she said shortly and Mr Birn chuckled.

"You're a fool," he said frankly.

"I wish I were no worse than that," said Elsie Chaucer bitterly. "You don't want me any more, Mr Birn?"

"Sit down," he ordered. "Who did you find tonight?"

For a moment she did not reply.

"The man whom Welby introduced last night," she said.

"The South American?" Mr Birn pulled a long face. "He wasn't very profitable. I suppose you know that? We lost about four thousand pounds."

"Less the ring," said the girl.

"The ring he gave you? Well, that's worth about a hundred, and I'll be lucky to get sixty for it," said Mr Birn with a shrug. "You can keep that ring if you like."

"No thank you, Mr Birn," said the girl quietly. "I don't want those kind of presents."

"Come here," said Birn suddenly, and reluctantly she came round the table and stood before him.

He rose and took her hand.

"Elsie," he said, "I've got very fond of you and I've been a good friend of yours, you know. If it hadn't been for me what would have happened to your father? He'd have been hung! That would have been nice for you, wouldn't it?"

She did not reply but gently disengaged her hand.

"You needn't put away those jewels and fine clothes every night, if you're sensible," he went on, "and – "

"Happily I am sensible, if by sensible you mean sane," said the girl, "and now I think I'll go if you don't mind, Mr Birn. I'm rather tired."

"Wait," he said.

He walked to the safe, unlocked it again and took out an oblong parcel wrapped in brown paper, fastened with tapes and sealed.

"There's a diamond necklace inside there," he said. "It's worth eight thousand pounds if it's worth a penny. I'm going to put it in my strong box at the bank tomorrow, unless – "

"Unless – " repeated the girl steadily.

"Unless you want it," said Mr Birn. "I'm a fool with the ladies."

She shook her head.

"Does it occur to you, Mr Birn," she said quietly, "that I could have had many necklaces if I wanted them. No, thank you. I am looking forward to the end of my servitude."

"And suppose I don't release you?" growled Mr Birn as he put back the package in the safe and locked the door. "Suppose I want you for another three years? How about that? Your father's still liable to arrest. No man can kill another, even if he's only a croupier, without hanging for it."

"I've paid for my father's folly, over and over again," said the girl in a low voice. "You don't know how I hate this life, Mr Birn. I feel worse than the worst woman in the world! I spend my life luring men to ruin – I wish to God I had never made the bargain. Sometimes I think I will tell my father just what I am paying for his safety, and let him decide whether my sacrifice is worth it."

A momentary look of alarm spread on the man's face.

"You'll do nothing of the kind," he said sharply. "Just as you've got into our ways! I was only joking about asking you to stay on. Now, my dear," he said with an air of banter, "you'd better go home and get your beauty sleep."

He walked with her to the door, saw her down the steps and watched her disappear in the darkness of the street, then he came back to lock up for the night. He drank up the half glass of whisky he had left and made a wry face.

"That's a queer taste," he said, took two steps towards the passage and fell in a heap.

The man who had slipped into the room when he had escorted Elsie Chaucer to the door came from behind the curtain and stooping loosened his collar. He stepped softly into the dimly lit passage and beckoned somebody, and Manfred came from the shadows, noiselessly, for he was wearing rubber over-boots.

Manfred glanced down at the unconscious man and then to the dregs in the whisky glass.

"Butyl chloride, I presume?"

"No more and no less," said the practical Leon, "in fact the 'knock-out-drop' which is so popular in criminal circles."

He searched the man, took out his keys, opened the safe and removing the sealed packet, he carried it to the table. Then he looked thoughtfully at the prostrate man.

"He will only be completely under the 'drop' for five minutes, Manfred, but I think that will be enough."

"Have you stopped to consider what will be the pathological results of 'twilight sleep' on top of butyl?" asked Manfred. "I saw you blending the hyocine with the morphia before we left Jermyn Street and I suppose that is what you are using?"

"I did not look it up," replied Gonsalez carelessly, "and if he dies, shall I weep? Give him another dose in half an hour, George. I will return by then."

He took from his pocket a small black case, and opened it; the hypodermic syringe it contained was already charged, and rolling back the man's sleeve, he inserted the needle and pressed home the piston.

Mr Birn woke the next morning with a throbbing headache.

He had no recollection of how he had got to bed, yet evidently he had undressed himself, for he was clad in his violet pyjamas. He rang the bell and got on to the floor, and though the room spun round him, he was able to hold himself erect.

The bell brought his housekeeper.

"What happened to me last night?" he asked, and she looked astounded.

"Nothing, sir. I left you in the library."

"It is that beastly whisky," grumbled Mr Birn.

A cold bath and a cup of tea helped to dissipate the headache, but he was still shaky when he went into the room in which he had been sitting the night before.

A thought had occurred to him. A terrifying thought. Suppose the whisky had been drugged (though what opportunity there had been for drugging his drink he could not imagine) and somebody had broken in!...

He opened the safe and breathed a sigh of relief. The package was still there. It must have been the whisky, he grumbled, and declining breakfast, he ordered his car and was driven straight to the bank.

When he reached his office, he found the hatchet-faced young man in a state of agitation.

"I think we must have had burglars here last night, Mr Birn."

"Burglars?" said Mr Birn alarmed. And then with a laugh, "well, they wouldn't get much here. But what makes you think they have been?"

"Somebody has been in the room, that I'll swear," said the young man. "The safe was open when I came and one of the books had been taken out and left on your table."

A slow smile dawned on Mr Birn's face.

"I wish them luck," he said.

Nevertheless he was perturbed, and made a careful search of all his papers to see if any important documents had been abstracted. His promissory notes were at the bank, in that same large box wherein was deposited the necklace which had come to him for the settlement of a debt.

Just before noon his clerk came in quickly.

"That fellow is here," he whispered.

"Which fellow?" growled Mr Birn.

"The man from Jermyn Street who stopped the payment of Eden's cheques."

"Ask him in," said Mr Birn. "Well, sir," he said jovially, "have you thought better about settling those debts?"

"Better and better," said Gonsalez. "I can speak to you alone, I suppose?"

Birn signalled his assistant to leave them.

"I've come to settle all sorts of debts. For example, I've come to settle the debt of a gentleman named Chaucer."

The gambling-house keeper started.

"A very charming fellow, Chaucer. I've been interviewing him this morning. Some time ago he had a shock which brought on a stroke of paralysis. He's not been able to leave his room in consequence for some time."

"You're telling me a lot I don't want to hear about," said Mr Brin briskly.

"The poor fellow is under the impression that he killed a red-haired croupier of yours. Apparently he was gambling and lost his head, when he saw your croupier taking a bill."

"My croupier," said the other with virtuous indignation. "What do you mean? I don't know what a croupier is."

"He hit him over the head with a money-rake. You came to Chaucer the next day and told him your croupier was dead, seeking to extract money from him. You soon found he was ruined. You found also he had a very beautiful daughter, and it occurred to you that she might be of use to you in your nefarious schemes, so you had a little talk with her and she agreed to enter your service in order to save her father from ruin and possibly imprisonment."

"This is a fairy story you're telling me, is it?" said Birn, but his face had gone a pasty white and the hand that took the cigar from his lips trembled.

"To bolster up your scheme," Gonsalez went on, "you inserted an advertisement in the death column of *The Times* and also you sent to the local newspaper a very flowery account of Mr Jinkins' funeral, which was also intended for Chaucer and his daughter."

"It's Greek to me," murmured Mr Birn with a pathetic attempt at a smile.

"I interviewed Mr Chaucer this morning and was able to assure him that Jinkins is very much alive and is living at Brighton, and is running a little gambling-house – a branch of your many activities, and by the way, Mr Birn, I don't think you will see Elsie Chaucer again."

Birn was breathing heavily.

"You know a hell of a lot," he began, but something in Leon's eyes stopped him.

"Birn," said Gonsalez softly. "I am going to ruin you – to take away every penny of the money you have stolen from the foolish men who patronise your establishments."

"Try it on," said Birn shakily. "There's a law in this country! Go and rob the bank, and you'd have little to rob," he added with a grin. "There's two hundred thousand pounds' worth of securities in my bank – gilt-edged ones, Mr Clever! Go and ask the bank manager to hand them over to you. They're in Box 65," he jeered. "That's the only way you can ruin me, my son."

Leon rose with a shrug.

"Perhaps I'm wrong," he said. "Perhaps after all you will enjoy your ill-gotten gains."

"You bet your life I will." Mr Birn relit his cigar.

He remembered the conversation that afternoon when he received an urgent telephone message from the bank. What the manager said took him there as fast as a taxi could carry him.

"I don't know what's the matter with your strong box," said the bank manager, "but one of my clerks who had to go into the vault said there was an extraordinary smell, and when we looked at the box, we found a stream of smoke coming through the keyhole."

"Why didn't you open it?" screamed Birn, fumbling for his key.

"Partly because I haven't a key, Mr Birn," said the bank manager intelligently.

With shaking hands the financier inserted the key and threw back the lid. A dense cloud of acrid yellow smoke came up and nearly stifled him...all that remained of his perfectly good securities was a black, sticky mess; a glass bottle, a few dull gems and nothing...

"It looks to me," said the detective officer who investigated the circumstance, "as though you must have inadvertently put in a package containing a very strong acid. What the acid is our analysts are working on now. It must have either leaked out or burst."

"The only package there," wailed Mr Birn, "was a package containing a diamond necklace."

"The remnants of which are still there," said the detective. "You are quite sure nobody could get at that package and substitute a destroying agent? It could easily be made. A bottle such as we found – a stopper made of some easily consumed material and there you are! Could anybody have opened the package and slipped the bottle inside?"

"Impossible, impossible," moaned the financier.

He was sitting with his face in his hands, weeping for his lost affluence, for though a few of the contents of that box could be replaced, there were certain American bonds which had gone forever and promissory notes by the thousand which would never be signed again.

THE MAN WHO WOULD NOT SPEAK

But for the fact that he was already the possessor of innumerable coats-of-arms, quarterings, family mottoes direct and affiliated, Leon Gonsalez might have taken for his chief motto the tag *homo sum, nihil humani a me alienum puto*. For there was no sphere of human activity which did not fascinate him. Wherever crowds gathered, wherever man in the aggregate was to be seen at his best or worst, there was Gonsalez to be found, oblivious to the attractions which had drawn the throng together, intensely absorbed in the individual members of the throng themselves.

Many years ago four young men, wealthy and intensely sincere, had come together with a common purpose inspired by one common ideal. There had been, and always will be, such combinations of enthusiasts. Great religious revivals, the creation of missions and movements of sociological reform, these and other developments have resulted from the joining together of fiery young zealots.

But the Four Just Men had as their objective the correction of the law's inequalities. They sought and found the men whom the wide teeth of the legal rake had left behind, and they dealt out their justice with terrible swiftness.

None of the living three (for one had died at Bordeaux) had departed from their ideals, but it was Leon who retained the appearance of that youthful enthusiasm which had brought them together.

He sought for interests in all manner of places, and it was at the back of the grandstand at Hurst Park racecourse that he first saw

"Spaghetti" Jones. It is one of the clear laws of coincidence, that if, in reading a book, you come across a word which you have not seen before, and which necessitates a reference to the dictionary, that same word will occur within three days on some other printed page. This law of the Inexplicable Recurrences applies equally to people, and Leon, viewing the hulk of the big man, had a queer feeling that they were destined to meet again – Leon's instincts were seldom at fault.

Mr Spaghetti Jones was a tall, strong and stoutly built man, heavy eyed and heavy jawed. He had a long dark moustache which curled at the ends, and he wore a green and white bow tie that the startling pink of his shirt might not be hidden from the world. There were diamond rings on his fat fingers, and a cable chain across his figured waistcoat. He was attired in a very bright blue suit, perfectly tailored, and violently yellow boots encased his feet, which were small for a man of his size. In fact, Mr Spaghetti Jones was a model of what Mr Spaghetti Jones thought a gentleman should be.

It was not his rich attire, nor his greatness of bulk, which ensured for him Leon's fascinated interest. Gonsalez had strolled to the back of the stand whilst the race was in progress, and the paddock was empty. Empty save for Mr Jones and two men, both smaller and both more poorly dressed than he.

Leon had taken a seat near the ring where the horses paraded, and it happened that the party strolled towards him. Spaghetti Jones made no attempt to lower his voice. It was rich and full of volume, and Leon heard every word. One of the men appeared to be quarrelling: the other, after a vain attempt to act as arbitrator, had subsided into silence.

"I told you to be at Lingfield, and you weren't there," Mr Jones was saying gently.

He was cleaning his nails with a small penknife Leon saw, and apparently his attention was concentrated on the work of beautification.

"I'm not going to Lingfield, or to anywhere else for you, Jones," said the man angrily.

He was a sharp, pale-faced man, and Leon knew from the note in his voice that he was frightened, and was employing this blustering manner to hide his fear.

"Oh, you're not going to Lingfield or anywhere else, aren't you?" repeated Spaghetti Jones.

He pushed his hat to the back of his head, and raised his eyes momentarily, and then resumed his manicuring.

"I've had enough of you and your crowd," the man went on. "We're blooming slaves, that's what we are! I can make more money running alone, now do you see?"

"I see," said Jones. "But, Tom, I want you to be at Sandown next Thursday. Meet me in the ring – "

"I won't, I won't," roared the other, red of face. "I've finished with you, and all your crowd!"

"You're a naughty boy," said Spaghetti Jones almost kindly.

He slashed twice at the other's face with his little penknife, and the man jumped back with a cry.

"You're a naughty boy," said Jones, returning to the contemplation of his nails, "and you'll be at Sandown when I tell you."

With that he turned and walked away.

The man called Tom pulled out a handkerchief and dabbed his bleeding face. There were two long shallow gashes – Mr Jones knew to an nth of an inch how deeply he could go in safety – but they were ugly and painful.

The wounded man glared after the retreating figure, and showed his discoloured teeth in an ugly grin, but Leon knew that he would report for duty at Sandown as he was ordered.

The sight was immensely interesting to Leon Gonsalez.

He came back to the flat in Jermyn Street full of it.

Manfred was out visiting his dentist, but the moment he came into the doorway Leon babbled forth his discovery.

"Absolutely the most amazing fellow I've seen in my life, George!" he cried enthusiastically. "A gorgeous atavism – a survival of the age of cruelty such as one seldom meets. You remember that shepherd we found at Escorial? He was the nearest, I think. This man's name is

Spaghetti Jones," he went on, "he is the leader of a racecourse gang which blackmails bookmakers. His nickname is derived from the fact that he has Italian blood and lives in the Italian quarter, and I should imagine from the general asymmetry of the face, and the fullness of his chin, that there is a history of insanity, and certainly epilepsy, on the maternal side of his family."

Manfred did not ask how Leon had made these discoveries. Put Leon on the track of an interesting "subject" and he would never leave it until it was dissected fibre by fibre and laid bare for his examination.

"He has a criminal record – I suppose?"

Gonsalez laughed, delighted.

"That is where you're wrong, my dear Manfred. He has never been convicted, and probably never will be. I found a poor little bookmaker in the silver ring – the silver ring is the enclosure where smaller bets are made than in Tattersall's reservation – who has been paying tribute to Caesar for years. He was a little doleful and maudlin, otherwise he would not have told me what he did. I drove him to a public-house in Cobham, far from the madding crowd, and he drank gin (which is the most wholesome drink obtainable in this country, if people only knew it) until he wept, and weeping unbuttoned his soul."

Manfred smiled and rang the bell for dinner.

"The law will lay him low sooner or later: I have a great faith in English law," he said. "It misses far fewer times than any other law that is administered in the world."

"But will it?" said Leon doubtfully.

"I'd like to talk with the courteous Mr Fare about this gentleman."

"You'll have an opportunity," said Manfred, "for we are dining with him tomorrow night at the Metropolitan Restaurant."

Their credentials as Spanish criminologists had served them well with Mr Fare and they in turn had assisted him – and Fare was thankful.

It was after the Sunday night dinner, when they were smoking their cigars, and most of the diners at the Metropolitan had strayed out into the dancing-room, that Leon told his experience.

Fare nodded.

"Oh yes, Spaghetti Jones is a hard case," he said. "We have never been able to get him, although he has been associated with some pretty unpleasant crimes. The man is colossal. He is brilliantly clever, in spite of his vulgarity and lack of education: he is remorseless, and he rules his little kingdom with a rod of iron. We have never been able to get one man to turn informer against him, and certainly he has never yet been caught with the goods."

He flicked the ash of his cigar into his saucer, and looked a long time thoughtfully at the grey heap.

"In America the Italians have a Black Hand organisation. I suppose you know that? It is a system of blackmail, the operations of which, happily, we have not seen in this country. At least, we hadn't seen it until quite recently. I have every reason to believe that Spaghetti Jones is the guiding spirit in the one authentic case which has been brought to our notice."

"Here in London?" said Manfred in surprise. "I hadn't the slightest idea they tried that sort of thing in England."

The Commissioner nodded.

"It may, of course, be a fake, but I've had some of my best men on the track of the letter-writers for a month, without getting any nearer to them. I was only wondering this morning, as I was dressing, whether I could not interest you gentlemen in a case where I confess we are a little at sea. Do you know the Countess Vinci?"

To Leon's surprise Manfred nodded.

"I met her in Rome, about three years ago," he said. "She is the widow of Count Antonio Vinci, is she not?"

"She is a widow with a son aged nine," said the Commissioner, "and she lives in Berkeley Square. A very wealthy lady and extremely charming. About two months ago she began to receive letters, which had no signature, but in its stead, a black cross. They were written in beautiful script writing, and that induced a suspicion of Spaghetti Jones who, in his youth, was a sign-writer."

Leon nodded his head vigorously.

"Of course, it is impossible to identify that kind of writing," he said admiringly. "By 'script' I suppose you mean writing which is actually printed? That is a new method, and a particularly ingenious one, but I interrupted you, sir. Did these letters ask for money?"

"They asked for money and threatened the lady as to what would happen if she failed to send to an address which was given. And here the immense nerve of Jones and his complicity was shown. Ostensibly Jones carries on the business of a newsagent. He has a small shop in Notting Hill, where he sells the morning and evening papers, and is a sort of local agent for racing tipsters whose placards you sometimes see displayed outside newspaper shops. In addition, the shop is used as an accommodation address – "

"Which means," said Manfred, "that people who do not want their letters addressed to their houses can have them sent there?"

The Commissioner nodded.

"They charge twopence a letter. These accommodation addresses should, of course, be made illegal, because they open the way to all sorts of frauds. The cleverness of the move is apparent: Jones receives the letter, ostensibly on behalf of some client, the letter is in his hands, he can open it or leave it unopened so that if the police call – as we did on one occasion – there is the epistle intact! Unless we prevent it reaching his shop we are powerless to keep the letter under observation. As a matter of fact, the name of the man to whom the money was to be sent, according to the letter which the Countess received, was 'H Frascati, care of John Jones'. Jones, of course, received the answer to the Countess's letter, put the envelope with dozens of other letters which were waiting to be claimed, and when our man went in in the evening, after having kept observation of the shop all day, he was told that the letter had been called for, and as, obviously, he could not search everybody who went in and out of the shop in the course of the day, it was impossible to prove the man's guilt."

"A wonderful scheme!" said the admiring Gonsalez. "Did the Countess send money?"

"She sent £200 very foolishly," said Fare with a shake of his head, "and then when the next demand came she informed the police. A trap letter was made up and sent to Jones's address, with the result as I have told you. She received a further note, demanding immediate payment, and threatening her and her boy, and a further trap letter was sent; this was last Thursday: and from a house on the opposite side of the road two of our officers kept observation, using field-glasses, which gave them a view of the interior of the shop. No letter was handed over during the day by Jones, so in the evening we raided the premises, and there was that letter on the shelf with others, unopened, and we looked extremely foolish," said the Commissioner with a smile. He thought awhile. "Would you like to meet the Countess Vinci?" he asked.

"Very much indeed," said Gonsalez quickly, and looked at his watch.

"Not tonight," smiled the Commissioner. "I will fix an interview for you tomorrow afternoon. Possibly you two ingenious gentlemen may think of something which has escaped our dull British wits."

On their way back to Jermyn Street that night, Leon Gonsalez broke the silence with a startling question.

"I wonder where one could get an empty house with a large bathroom and a very large bath?" he asked thoughtfully.

"Why ever – ?" began Manfred, and then laughed. "I'm getting old, I think, Leon," he said as they turned into the flat. "There was a time when the amazing workings of your mind did not in any way surprise me. What other characteristics must this ideal home of yours possess?"

Leon scientifically twirled his hat across the room so that it fell neatly upon a peg of the hat-rack.

"How is that for dexterity, George?" he asked in self-admiration. "The house – oh well, it ought to be a little isolated, standing by itself in its own grounds, if possible. Well away from the road, and the road not often frequented. I should prefer that it was concealed from observation by bushes or trees."

"It sounds as if you're contemplating a hideous crime," said Manfred good-humouredly.

"Not I," corrected Leon quickly, "but I think our friend Jones is a real nasty fellow." He heaved a big sigh. "I'd give anything for his head measurements," he said inconsequently.

Their interview with the Countess Vinci was a pleasant one. She was a tall, pretty woman, of thirty-four, the "grande dame" to her fingertips.

Manfred, who was human, was charmed by her, for Leon Gonsalez, she was too normal to be really interesting.

"Naturally I'm rather worried," she said. "Philip is not very strong, though he's not delicate."

Later the boy came in, a straight, little fellow with an olive skin and brown eyes, self-possessed and more intelligent than Manfred had expected from his years. With him was his governess, a pretty Italian girl.

"I trust Beatrice more than I trust your police," said the Countess when the girl had taken her charge back to his lessons. "Her father is an officer in the Sicilian police, and she has lived practically all her life under threat of assassination."

"Does the boy go out?" asked Manfred.

"Once a day, in the car," said the Countess. "Either I take him or Beatrice and I, or Beatrice alone."

"Exactly what do they threaten?" asked Gonsalez.

"I will show you one of their letters," said the Countess.

She went to a bureau, unlocked it, and came back with a stout sheet of paper. It was of excellent quality and the writing was in copper-plate characters:

"You will send us a thousand pounds on the first of March, June, September and December. The money should be in bank-notes and should be sent to H Frascati, care of J Jones, 194 Notting Hill Crescent. It will cost you more to get your boy back than it will cost you to keep him with you."

Gonsalez held the paper to the light, then carried it to the window for a better examination.

"Yes," he said as he handed it back. "It would be difficult to trace the writer of that. The best expert in the world would fail."

"I suppose you can suggest nothing," said the Countess, shaking her head in anticipation, as they rose to go.

She spoke to Manfred, but it was Gonsalez who answered.

"I can only suggest, madame," he said, "that if your little boy does disappear you communicate with us immediately."

"And my dear Manfred," he said when they were in the street, "that Master Philip *will* disappear is absolutely certain. I'm going to take a cab and drive round London looking for that house of mine."

"Are you serious, Leon?" asked Manfred, and the other nodded.

"Never more serious in my life," he said soberly. "I will be at the flat in time for dinner."

It was nearly eight o'clock, an hour after dinner-time, when he came running up the stairs of the Jermyn Street establishment, and burst into the room.

"I have got – " he began, and then saw Manfred's face. "Have they taken him?"

Manfred nodded.

"I had a telephone message an hour ago," he said.

Leon whistled.

"So soon," he was speaking to himself. And then: "How did it happen?"

"Fare has been here. He left just before you came," said Manfred. "The abduction was carried out with ridiculous ease. Soon after we left, the governess took the boy out in the car, and they followed their usual route, which is across Hampstead Heath to the country beyond. It is their practice to go a few miles beyond the Heath in the direction of Beacon's Hill and then to turn back."

"Following the same route every day was, of course, sheer lunacy," said Leon. "Pardon me."

"The car always turns at the same point," said Manfred, "and that is the fact which the abductors had learnt. The road is not especially wide, and to turn the big Rolls requires a little manoeuvring. The chauffeur was engaged in bringing the car round, when a man rode up on a bicycle, a pistol was put under the chauffeur's nose, and at the same time two men, appearing from nowhere, pulled open the door of the car, snatched away the revolver which the governess carried, and carried the screaming boy down the road to another car, which the driver of the Vinci car had seen standing by the side of the road, but which apparently had not aroused his suspicion."

"The men's faces, were they seen?"

Manfred shook his head.

"The gentleman who held up the chauffeur wore one of those cheap theatrical beards which you can buy for a shilling at any toyshop, and in addition a pair of motor goggles. Both the other men seemed to be similarly disguised. I was just going to the Countess when you came. If you'll have your dinner, Leon – "

"I want no dinner," said Leon promptly.

Commissioner Fare was at the house in Berkeley Square when they called, and he was endeavouring vainly to calm the distracted mother.

He hailed the arrival of the two men with relief.

"Where is the letter?" said Leon immediately he entered the room.

"What letter?"

"The letter they have sent stating their terms."

"It hasn't arrived yet," said the other in a low voice. "Do you think that you can calm the Countess? She is on the verge of hysteria."

She was lying on a sofa deathly white, her eyes closed, and two maidservants were endeavouring to rouse her. She opened her eyes at Manfred's voice, and looked up.

"Oh my boy, my boy?" she sobbed, and clasped his hands in both of hers. "You will get him back, please. I will give anything, anything. You cannot name a sum that I will not pay!"

It was then that the butler came into the room bearing a letter on a salver.

She sprang up, but would have fallen had not Manfred's arm steadied her.

"It is from – them," she cried wildly and tore open the envelope with trembling fingers.

The message was a longer one:

"Your son is in a place which is known only to the writer. The room is barred and locked and contains food and water sufficient to last for four days. None but the writer knows where he is or can find him. For the sum of twenty-five thousand pounds his hiding place will be sent to the Countess, and if that sum is not forthcoming, he will be left to starve."

"I must send the money immediately," cried the distraught lady. "Immediately! Do you understand? My boy – my boy!…"

"Four days," murmured Leon, and his eyes were bright. "Why it couldn't be better!"

Only Manfred heard him.

"Madam," said Mr Fare gravely, "if you send twenty-five thousand pounds what assurance have you that the boy will be restored? You are a very rich woman. Is it not likely that this man, when he gets your money, will make a further demand upon you?"

"Besides which," interrupted Leon, "it would be a waste of money. I will undertake to restore your boy in two days. Perhaps in one, it depends very much upon whether Spaghetti Jones sat up late last night."

Mr Spaghetti Jones was nicknamed partly because of his association with the sons and daughters of Italy, and partly because, though a hearty feeder, he invariably finished his dinner, however many courses he might have consumed, with the Italian national dish.

He had dined well at his favourite restaurant in Soho, sitting aloof from the commonplace diners, and receiving the obsequious services of the restaurant proprietor with a complacency which suggested that it was no more than his right.

He employed a toothpick openly, and then paying his bill, he sauntered majestically forth and hailed a taxicab. He was on the point of entering it when two men closed in, one on each side of him.

"Jones," said one sharply.

"That's my name," said Mr Jones.

"I am Inspector Jetheroe from Scotland Yard, and I shall take you into custody on a charge of abducting Count Philip Vinci."

Mr Jones stared at him.

Many attempts had been made to bring him to the inhospitable shelter which His Majesty's Prisons afford, and they had all failed.

"You have made a bloomer, haven't you?" he chuckled, confident in the efficiency of his plans.

"Get into that cab," said the man shortly, and Mr Jones was too clever and experienced a juggler with the law to offer any resistance.

Nobody would betray him – nobody could discover the boy, he had not exaggerated in that respect. The arrest meant no more than a visit to the station, a few words with the inspector and at the worst a night's detention.

One of his captors had not entered the cab until he had a long colloquy with the driver, and Mr Jones, seeing through the window the passing of a five-pound note, wondered what mad fit of generosity had overtaken the police force.

They drove rapidly through the West End, down Whitehall, and to Mr Jones's surprise, did not turn into Scotland Yard, but continued over Westminster Bridge.

"Where are you taking me?" he asked.

The man who sat opposite him, the smaller man who had spoken to the cabman, leant forward and pushed something into Mr Jones's ample waistcoat, and glancing down he saw the long black barrel of an automatic pistol, and he felt a momentary sickness.

"Don't talk – yet," said the man.

Try as he did, Jones could not see the face of either detective. Passing, however, under the direct rays of an electric lamp, he had a shock. The face of the man opposite him was covered by a thin white veil which revealed only the vaguest outlines of a face. And then he began to think rapidly. But the solutions to his difficulties came back to that black and shining pistol in the other's hands.

On through New Cross, Lewisham, and at last the cab began the slow descent of Blackheath Hill. Mr Jones recognised the locality as one in which he had operated from time to time with fair success.

The cab reached the Heath Road, and the man who was sitting by his side opened the window and leant out, talking to the driver. Suddenly the car turned through the gateway of a garden and stopped before the uninviting door of a gaunt, deserted house.

"Before you get out," said the man with the pistol, "I want you to understand that if you talk or shout or make any statement to the driver of this cab, I shall shoot you through the stomach. It will take you about three days to die, and you will suffer pains which I do not think your gross mind can imagine."

Mr Jones mounted the steps to the front door and passed meekly and in silence into the house. The night was chilly and he shivered as he entered the comfortless dwelling. One of the men switched on an electric lamp, by the light of which he locked the door. Then he put the light out, and they found their way up the dusty stairs with the assistance of a pocket lamp which Leon Gonsalez flashed before him.

"Here's your little home," said Leon pleasantly, and opening the door, turned a switch.

It was a big bathroom. Evidently Leon had found his ideal, thought Manfred, for the room was unusually large, so large that a bed could be placed in one corner, and had been so placed by Mr Gonsalez. George Manfred saw that his friend had had a very busy day. The bed was a comfortable one, and with its white sheets and soft pillows looked particularly inviting.

In the bath, which was broad and deep, a heavy Windsor chair had been placed, and from one of the taps hung a length of rubber hosing.

These things Mr Jones noticed, and also marked the fact that the window had been covered with blankets to exclude the light.

"Put out your hands," said Leon sharply, and before Spaghetti Jones realised what was happening, a pair of handcuffs had been snapped on his wrists, a belt had been deftly buckled through the connecting links, and drawn between his legs.

"Sit down on that bed. I want you to see how comfortable is it," said Leon humorously.

"I don't know what you think you're doing," said Mr Jones in a sudden outburst of rage, "but by God you'll know all about it! Take that veil off your face and let me see you."

"I'd rather you didn't," said Leon gently. "If you saw my face I should be obliged to kill you, and that I have no desire to do. Sit down."

Mr Jones obeyed wonderingly, and his wonder increased when Leon began to strip his patent shoes and silk socks, and to roll up the legs of his trousers.

"What is the game?" asked the man fearfully.

"Get on to that chair." Gonsalez pointed to the chair in the bath. "It is an easy Windsor chair – "

"Look here," began Jones fearfully.

"Get in," snapped Leon, and the big fellow obeyed.

"Are you comfortable?" asked Leon politely.

The man glowered at him.

"You'll be uncomfortable before I'm through with you," he said.

"How do you like the look of that bed?" asked Leon. "It looks rather cosy, eh?"

Spaghetti Jones did not answer, and Gonsalez tapped him lightly on the shoulder.

"Now, my gross friend, will you tell me where you have hidden Philip Vinci?"

"Oh, that is it, is it?" grinned Mr Jones. "Well, you can go on asking!"

He glared down at his bare feet, and then from one to the other of the two men.

"I don't know anything about Philip Vinci," he said. "Who is he?"

"Where have you hidden Philip Vinci?"

"You don't suppose if I knew where he was I'd tell you, do you?" sneered Jones.

"If you know, you certainly will tell me," answered Leon quietly, "but I fancy it is going to be a long job. Perhaps in thirty-six hours' time? George, will you take the first watch? I'm going to sleep on that very comfortable bed, but first," he groped at the back of the bath and found a strap and this he passed round the body of his prisoner, buckling it behind the chair, "to prevent you falling off," he said pleasantly.

He lay down on the bed and in a few minutes was fast asleep. Leon had that gift of sleeping at will, which has ever been the property of great commanders.

Jones looked from the sleeper to the veiled man who lounged in an easy chair facing him. Two eyes were cut in the veil, and the watcher had a book on his knee and was reading.

"How long is this going on?" he demanded.

"For a day or two," said Manfred calmly. "Are you very much bored? Would you like to read?"

Mr Jones growled something unpleasant, and did not accept the offer. He could only think and speculate upon what their intentions were. He had expected violence, but apparently no violence was intended. They were merely keeping him prisoner till he spoke. But he would show them! He began to feel tired. Suddenly his head drooped forward, till his chin touched his breast.

"Wake up," said Manfred shortly.

He awoke with a start.

"You're not supposed to sleep," explained Manfred.

"Ain't I?" growled the prisoner. "Well, I'm going to sleep!" and he settled himself more easily in the chair.

He was beginning to doze when he experienced an acute discomfort and drew up his feet with a yell. The veiled man was directing a stream of ice-cold water upon his unprotected feet, and Mr Jones was now thoroughly awake. An hour later he was nodding again, and again the tiny hose-pipe was directed to his feet, and again Manfred produced a towel and dried them as carefully as though Mr Jones were an invalid.

At six o'clock in the morning, red-eyed and glaring, he watched Manfred rouse the sleeping Leon and take his place on the bed.

Again and again nature drew the big man's chin down to his chest, and again and again the icy stream played maddeningly upon him and he woke with a scream.

"Let me sleep, let me sleep!" he cried in helpless rage, tugging at the strap. He was half-mad with weariness, his eyes were like lead.

"Where is Philip Vinci," demanded the inexorable Leon.

"This is torture, damn you – " screamed the man.

"No worse for you than for the boy locked up in a room with four days' supply of food. No worse than slitting a man's face with a penknife, my primitive friend. But perhaps you do not think it is a serious matter to terrify a little child."

"I don't know where he is, I tell you," said Spaghetti hoarsely.

"Then we shall have to keep you awake till you remember," replied Leon, and lit a cigarette.

Soon after he went downstairs and returned with coffee and biscuits for the man, and found him sleeping soundly.

His dreams ended in a wail of agony.

"Let me sleep, please let me sleep," he begged with tears in his eyes. "I'll give you anything if you'll let me sleep!"

"You can sleep on that bed – and it's a very comfortable bed too – " said Leon, "but first we shall learn where Philip Vinci is."

"I'll see you in hell before I'll tell you," screamed Spaghetti Jones.

"You will wear your eyes out looking for me," answered Leon politely. "Wake up!"

At seven o'clock that evening a weeping, whimpering, broken man, moaned an address, and Manfred went off to verify this information.

"Now let me sleep!"

"You can keep awake till my friend comes back," said Leon.

At nine o'clock George Manfred returned from Berkeley Square, having released a frightened little boy from a very unpleasant cellar in Notting Hill, and together they lifted the half-dead man from the bath and unlocked the handcuffs.

"Before you sleep, sit here," said Manfred, "and sign this."

"This" was a document which Mr Jones could not have read even if he had been willing. He scrawled his signature, and crawling on to the bed was asleep before Manfred pulled the clothes over him. And he was still asleep when a man from Scotland Yard came into the room and shook him violently.

Spaghetti Jones knew nothing of what the detective said; had no recollection of being charged or of hearing his signed confession read over to him by the station sergeant. He remembered nothing until they woke him in his cell to appear before the magistrate for a preliminary hearing.

"It's an extraordinary thing, sir," said the gaoler to the divisional surgeon. "I can't get this man to keep awake."

"Perhaps he would like a cold bath," said the surgeon helpfully.

THE MAN WHO WAS ACQUITTED

"Have you ever noticed," said Leon Gonsalez, looking up from his book and taking off the horn-rimmed glasses he wore when he was reading, "that poisoners and baby-farmers are invariably mystics?"

"I haven't noticed many baby-farmers – or poisoners for the matter of that," said Manfred with a little yawn. "Do you mean by 'mystic' an ecstatic individual who believes he can communicate directly with the Divine Power?"

Leon nodded.

"I've never quite understood the association of a superficial but vivid form of religion with crime," said Leon, knitting his forehead. "Religion, of course, does not develop the dormant criminality in a man's ethical system; but it is a fact that certain criminals develop a queer form of religious exaltation. Ferri, who questioned 200 Italian murderers, found that they were all devout: Naples, which is the most religious city in Europe, is also the most criminal. Ten per cent of those inmates of British prisons who are tattooed are marked with religious symbols."

"Which only means that when a man of low intelligence submits to the tattoo artist, he demands pictures of the things with which he is familiar," said Manfred, and took up the paper he was reading. Suddenly he dropped the journal on his knees.

"You're thinking of Dr Twenden," he said, and Leon inclined his head slowly.

"I was," he confessed.

Manfred smiled.

"Twenden was acquitted with acclamation and cheered as he left the Exeter Assize Court," he said, "and yet he was guilty!"

"As guilty as a man can be – I wondered if your mind was on the case, George. I haven't discussed it with you."

"By the way, was he religious?" asked Manfred.

"I wouldn't say that," said the other, shaking his head. "I was thinking of the pious letter of thanks he wrote, and which was published in the Baxeter and Plymouth newspapers – it was rather like a sermon. What he is in private life I know no more than the account of the trial told me. You think he poisoned his wife?"

"I am sure," said Manfred quietly. "I intended discussing the matter with you this evening."

The trial of Dr Twenden had provided the newspaper sensation of the week. The doctor was a man of thirty: his wife was seventeen years his senior and the suggestion was that he had married her for her money – she had a legacy of £2,000 a year which ceased at her death. Three months before this event she had inherited £63,000 from her brother, who had died in Johannesburg.

Twenden and his wife had not been on the best of terms, one of the subjects of disagreement being her unwillingness to continue paying his debts. After her inheritance had been transferred to her, she sent to Torquay, to her lawyer, the draft of a will in which she left the income from £12,000 to her husband, providing he did not marry again. The remainder of her fortune she proposed leaving to her nephew, one Jacley, a young civil engineer in the employ of the Plymouth Corporation.

The lawyer drafted her bequests and forwarded a rough copy for her approval before the will was engrossed. That draft arrived at Newton Abbot where the doctor and his wife were living (the doctor had a practice there) and was never seen again. A postman testified that it had been delivered at the 8 o'clock "round" on a Saturday. That day the doctor was called into consultation over a case of viper bite. He returned in the evening and dined with his wife. Nothing happened that was unusual. The doctor went to his laboratory to make an examination of the poison sac which had been extracted from the reptile.

In the morning Mrs Twenden was very ill, showed symptoms which could be likened to blood-poisoning and died the same night.

It was found that in her arm was a small puncture such as might be made by a hypodermic needle, such a needle as, of course, the doctor possessed – he had in fact ten.

Suspicion fell upon him immediately. He had not summoned any further assistance besides that which he could give, until all hope of saving the unfortunate woman had gone. It was afterwards proved that the poison from which the woman had died was snake venom.

In his favour was the fact that no trace of the poison was found in either of the three syringes or the ten needles in his possession. It was his practice, and this the servants and another doctor who had ordered the treatment testified, to give his wife a subcutaneous injection of a new serum for her rheumatism.

This he performed twice a week and on the Saturday the treatment was due.

He was tried and acquitted. Between the hour of his arrest and his release he had acquired the popularity which accumulates about the personality of successful politicians and good-looking murderers, and he had been carried from the Sessions House shoulder high through a mob of cheering admirers, who had discovered nothing admirable in his character, and were not even aware of his existence, till the iron hand of the law closed upon his arm.

Possibly the enthusiasm of the crowded was fanned to its high temperature by the announcement the accused man had made in the dock – he had defended himself.

"Whether I am convicted or acquitted, not one penny of my dear wife's money will I touch. I intend disposing of this accursed fortune to the poor of the country. I, for my part, shall leave this land for a distant shore and in a strange land, amidst strangers, I will cherish the memory of my dear wife, my partner and my friend."

Here the doctor broke down.

"A distant shore," said Manfred, recalling the prisoner's passionate words. "You can do a lot with sixty-three thousand pounds on a distant shore."

The eyes of Leon danced with suppressed merriment.

"It grieves me, George, to hear such cynicism. Have you forgotten that the poor of Devonshire are even now planning how the money will be spent?"

Manfred made a noise of contempt, and resumed his reading, but his companion had not finished with the subject.

"I should like to meet Twenden," he said reflectively. "Would you care to go to Newton Abbot, George? The town itself is not particularly beautiful, but we are within half an hour's run of our old home at Babbacome."

This time George Manfred put away his paper definitely.

"It was a particularly wicked crime," he said gravely. "I think I agree with you, Leon. I have been thinking of the matter all morning, and it seems to call for some redress. But," he hesitated, "it also calls for some proof. Unless we can secure evidence which did not come before the Court, we cannot act on suspicion."

Leon nodded.

"But if we prove it," he said softly, "I promise you, Manfred, a most wonderful scheme."

That afternoon he called upon his friend, Mr Fare of Scotland Yard, and when the Commissioner heard his request, he was less surprised than amused.

"I was wondering how long it would be before you wanted to see our prisons, Senor," he said. "I can arrange that with the Commissioners. What prison would you like to see?"

"I wish to see a typical county prison," said Leon. "What about Baxeter?"

"Baxeter," said the other in surprise. "That's rather a long way from London. It doesn't differ very materially from Wandsworth, which is a few miles from this building, or Pentonville, which is our headquarters prison."

"I prefer Baxeter," said Leon. "The fact is I am going to the Devonshire coast, and I could fill in my time profitably with this inspection."

The order was forthcoming on the next day. It was a printed note authorising the Governor of HM Prison, Baxeter, to allow the bearer to visit the prison between the hours of ten and twelve in the morning, and two and four in the afternoon.

They broke their journey at Baxeter, and Leon drove up to the prison, a prettier building than most of its kind. He was received by the Deputy Governor and a tall, good-looking chief warder, an ex-Guardsman, who showed him round the three wings, and through the restricted grounds of the gaol.

Leon rejoined his companion on the railway station just in time to catch the Plymouth express which would carry them to Newton Abbot.

"A thoroughly satisfactory visit," said Leon. "In fact, it is the most amazingly convenient prison I have ever been in."

"Convenient to get into or convenient to get away from?" asked Manfred.

"Both," said Leon.

They had not engaged rooms at either of the hotels. Leon had decided, if it was possible, to get lodgings near to the scene of the tragedy, and in this he was successful. Three houses removed from the corner house where Doctor Twenden was in residence, he discovered furnished lodgings were to let.

A kindly rosy-faced Devonshire woman was the landlady, and they were the only tenants, her husband being a gunner on one of His Majesty's ships, and he was at sea. She showed them a bright sitting-room and two bedrooms on the same floor. Manfred ordered tea, and when the door closed on the woman, he turned to behold Leon standing by the window gazing intently at the palm of his left hand, which was enclosed, as was the other, in a grey silk glove.

Manfred laughed.

"I don't usually make comments on your attire, my dear Leon," he said, "and remembering your Continental origin, it is remarkable that you commit so few errors in dress – from an Englishman's point of view," he added.

"It's queer, isn't it," said Leon, still looking at his palm.

"But I've never seen you wearing silk gloves before," Manfred went on curiously. "In Spain it is not unusual to wear cotton gloves, or even silk – "

"The finest silk," murmured Leon, "and I cannot bend my hand in it."

"Is that why you've been carrying it in your pocket," said Manfred in surprise, and Gonsalez nodded.

"I cannot bend my hand in it," he said, "because in the palm of my hand is a stiff copper-plate and on that plate is half an inch thickness of plastic clay of a peculiarly fine texture."

"I see," said Manfred slowly.

"I love Baxeter prison," said Leon, "and the Deputy Governor is a dear young man: his joy in my surprise and interest when he showed me the cells was delightful to see. He even let me examine the master key of the prison, which naturally he carried, and if, catching and holding his eye, I pressed the business end of the key against the palm of my gloved hand, why it was done in a second, my dear George, and there was nothing left on the key to show him the unfair advantage I had taken."

He had taken a pair of folding scissors from his pocket and dexterously had opened them and was soon cutting away the silk palm of the glove.

" 'How wonderful,' said I, 'and that is the master key!' and so we went on to see the punishment cell and the garden and the little unkempt graves where the dead men lie who have broken the law, and all the time I had to keep my hand in my pocket, for fear I'd knock against something and spoil the impression. Here it is."

The underside of the palm had evidently been specially prepared for the silk came off easily, leaving a thin grey slab of slate-coloured clay in the centre of which was clearly the impression of a key.

"The little hole at the side is where you dug the point of the key to get the diameter?" said Manfred, and Leon nodded.

"This is the master key of Baxeter Gaol, my dear Manfred," he said with a smile, as he laid it upon the table. "With this I could walk in — no, I couldn't." He stopped suddenly and bit his lip.

"You are colossal," said Manfred admiringly.

"Aren't I," said Leon with a wry face. "Do you know there is one door we can't open?"

"What is that?"

"The big gates outside. They can only be opened from the inside. H'm."

He laid his hat carefully over the clay mould when the landlady came in with the tray.

Leon sipped his tea, staring vacantly at the lurid wallpaper, and Manfred did not interrupt his thoughts.

Leon Gonsalez had ever been the schemer of the Four Just Men, and he had developed each particular of his plan as though it were a story he was telling himself. His extraordinary imagination enabled him to foresee every contingency. Manfred had often said that the making of the plan gave Leon as much pleasure as its successful consummation.

"What a stupid idiot I am," he said at last. "I didn't realise that there was no keyhole in the main gate of a prison — except of course Dartmoor."

Again he relapsed into silent contemplation of the wall, a silence broken by cryptic mutterings.

"I send the wire... It must come, of course, from London... They would send down if the wire was strong enough. It must be five men — no five could go into a taxi — six... If the door of the van is locked, but it won't be... If it fails then I could try the next night."

"What on earth are you talking about?" asked Manfred good-humouredly.

Leon woke with a start from his reverie.

"We must first prove that this fellow is guilty," he said, "and we'll have to start on that job tonight. I wonder if our good landlady has a garden."

The good landlady had one. It stretched out for two hundred yards at the back of the house, and Leon made a survey and was satisfied.

"The doctor's place?" he asked innocently, as the landlady pointed out this object of interest. "Not the man who was tried at Baxeter?"

"The very man," said the woman triumphantly. "I tell you, it caused a bit of a sensation round here."

"Do you think he was innocent?"

The landlady was not prepared to make a definite standpoint.

"Some think one thing and some think the other," she replied in the true spirit of diplomacy. "He's always been a nice man, and he attended my husband when he was home last."

"Is the doctor staying in his house?"

"Yes, sir," said the woman. "He's going abroad soon."

"Oh yes, he is distributing that money, isn't he? I read something about it in the newspapers – the poor are to benefit, are they not?"

The landlady sniffed.

"I hope they get it," she said significantly.

"Which means that you don't think they will," smiled Manfred, strolling back from an inspection of her early chrysanthemums.

"They may," said the cautious landlady, "but nothing has happened yet. The vicar went to the doctor yesterday morning, and asked him whether a little of it couldn't be spared for the poor of Newton Abbot. We've had a lot of unemployment here lately, and the doctor said 'Yes' he would think about it, and sent him a cheque for fifty pounds from what I heard."

"That's not a great deal," said Manfred. "What makes you think he is going abroad?"

"All his trunks are packed and his servants are under notice, that's how I came to know," said the landlady. "I don't think it's a bad thing. Poor soul, she didn't have a very happy life."

The "poor soul" referred to was apparently the doctor's wife, and when asked to explain, the landlady knew no more than that people had talked, that there was probably nothing in it, and why shouldn't the doctor go motoring on the moor with pretty girls if he felt that way inclined.

"He had his fancies," said the landlady.

Apparently those "fancies" came and went through the years of his married life.

"I should like to meet the doctor," said Leon, but she shook her head.

"He won't see anybody, not even his patients, sir," she said.

Nevertheless Leon succeeded in obtaining an interview. He had judged the man's character correctly thus far, and he knew he would not refuse an interview with a journalist.

The servant took Leon's name, closing the front door in his face while she went to see the doctor, and when she came back it was to invite him in.

He found the medical gentleman in his study, and the dismantled condition of the room supported Mrs Martin's statement that he was leaving the town at an early date. He was in fact engaged in destroying old business letters and bills when Leon arrived.

"Come in," grumbled the doctor. "I suppose if I didn't see you, you'd invent something about me. Now what do you want?"

He was a good-looking young man with regular features, a carefully trimmed black moustache and tiny black side-whiskers.

"Light-blue eyes I do not like," said Leon to himself, "and I should like to see you without a moustache."

"I've been sent down from London to ask to what charities you are distributing your wife's money, Dr Twenden," said Leon, with the brisk and even rude directness of a London reporter.

The doctor's lips curled.

"The least they can do is give me a chance to make up my mind," he said. "The fact is, I've got to go abroad on business, and whilst I'm away I shall carefully consider the merits of the various charity organisations of Devon to discover which are the most worthy and how the money is to be distributed."

"Suppose you don't come back again?" asked Leon cruelly. "I mean, anything might happen; the ship may sink or the train smash – what happens to the money then?"

"That is entirely my affair," said the doctor stiffly, and closing his eyes, arched his eyebrows for a second as he spoke. "I really don't wish to reopen this matter. I've had some very charming letters from the public, but I've had abusive ones too. I had one this morning saying that it was a pity that the Four Just Men were not in existence! The Four Just Men!" he smiled contemptuously, "as though I should have cared a snap of my fingers for that kind of cattle!"

Leon smiled too.

"Perhaps it would be more convenient if I saw you tonight," he suggested.

The doctor shook his head.

"I'm to be the guest of honour of a few friends of mine," he said, with a queer air of importance, "and I shan't be back until half past eleven at the earliest."

"Where is the dinner to be held? That might make an interesting item of news," said Leon.

"It's to be held at the Lion Hotel. You can say that Sir John Murden is in the chair, and that Lord Tussborough has promised to attend. I can give you the list of the people who'll be there."

"The dinner engagement is a genuine one," thought Leon with satisfaction.

The list was forthcoming, and pocketing the paper with due reverence, Gonsalez bowed himself out. From his bedroom window that evening he watched the doctor, splendidly arrayed, enter a taxi and drive away. A quarter of an hour later the servant, whom Leon had seen, came out pulling on her gloves. Gonsalez watched her for a good quarter of an hour, during which time she stood at the corner of the street. She was obviously waiting for something or somebody. What it was he saw. The Torquay bus passed by, stopped, and she mounted it.

After dinner he had a talk with the landlady and brought the conversation back to the doctor's house.

"I suppose it requires a lot of servants to keep a big house like that going?"

"He's only got one now, sir: Milly Brown, who lives in Torquay. She is leaving on Saturday. The cook left last week. The doctor has all his meals at the hotel."

He left Manfred to talk to the landlady – and Manfred could be very entertaining.

Slipping through the garden he reached a little alleyway at the back of the houses. The back gate giving admission to the doctor's garden was locked, but the wall was not high. He expected that the door of the house would be fastened, and he was not surprised when he found it was locked. A window by the side of the door was, however, wide open: evidently neither the doctor nor his maid expected burglars. He climbed through the window on to the kitchen sink, through the kitchen and into the house, without difficulty. His search of the library into which he had been shown that afternoon was a short one. The desk had no secret drawers, and most of the papers had been burnt. The ashes overflowed the grate on to the tiled hearth. The little laboratory, which had evidently been a creamery when the house was in former occupation, yielded nothing, nor did any of the rooms.

He had not expected that in this one search he would make a discovery, remembering that the police had probably ransacked the house after the doctor's arrest and had practically been in occupation ever since.

He went systematically and quickly through the pockets of all the doctor's clothing that he found in the wardrobe of his bedroom, but produced nothing more interesting than a theatre programme.

"I'm afraid I shan't want that key," said Leon regretfully, and went downstairs again. He turned on his pocket lamp: there might be other clothing hanging in the hall, but he found the rack was empty.

As he flashed the light around, the beam caught a large tin letter-box fastened to the door. He lifted up the yellow lid and at first saw nothing. The letter-box looked as if it had been homemade. It was, as he had seen at first, of grained and painted tin that had been shaped roughly round a wooden frame; he saw the supports at each corner. One was broken. He put in his hand, and saw that what he thought had been the broken ends of the frame, was a small square packet standing bolt upright: it was now so discoloured by dust that it seemed to be part of the original framework. He pulled it out, tearing the paper cover as he did so; it had been held in its place by the end of a nail which had been driven into the original wood, which explained why it had not fallen over when the door had been slammed. He blew the dust from it; the package was addressed from the Pasteur Laboratory. He had no desire to examine it there, and slipped it into his pocket, getting out of the house by the way he had come in, and rejoining Manfred just when that gentleman was beginning to get seriously worried, for Leon had been three hours in the house.

"Did you find anything?" asked Manfred when they were alone.

"This," said Leon. He pulled the packet out of his pocket and explained where he had found it.

"The Pasteur Institute," said Manfred in surprise. "Of course," he said suddenly, "the serum which the doctor used to inject into his wife's arm. Pasteur are the only people who prepare that. I remember reading as much in the account of the trial."

"And which he injected twice a week, if I remember rightly," said Leon, "on Wednesdays and Saturdays, and the evidence was that he did not inject it on the Wednesday before the murder. It struck me at the time as being rather curious that nobody asked him when he was in the witness box why he had omitted this injection."

He cut along the paper and pulled it apart: inside was an oblong wooden box, about which was wrapped a letter. It bore the heading of the laboratory, directions, and was in French:

"Sir (it began),
"We despatch to you immediately the serum Number 47 which you desire, and we regret that through the fault of a subordinate, this was not sent you last week. We received your telegram today that you are entirely without serum, and we will endeavour to expedite the delivery of this."

"Entirely without serum," repeated Gonsalez. He took up the wrapping-paper and examined the stamp. "Paris, the 14th September," he said, "and here's the receiving stamp, Newton Abbot the 16th September, 7 a.m."

He frowned.

"This was pushed through the letter-box on the morning of the 16th," he said slowly. "Mrs Twenden was injected on the evening of the 15th. The 16th was a Sunday, and there's an early post. Don't you see, Manfred?"

Manfred nodded.

"Obviously he could not have injected serum because he had none to inject, and this arrived when his wife was dying. It is, of course, untouched."

He took out a tiny tube and tapped the seal.

"H'm," said Leon, "I shall want that key after all. Do you remember, Manfred, he did not inject on Wednesday: why? Because he had no serum. He was expecting the arrival of this, and it must have gone out of his mind. Probably we shall discover that the postman knocked, and getting no answer on the Sunday morning, pushed the little package through the letter-box, where by accident it must have fallen into the corner where I discovered it."

He put down the paper and drew a long breath.

"And now I think I will get to work on that key," he said.

Two days later Manfred came in with news.

"Where is my friend?"

Mrs Martin, the landlady, smiled largely.

"The gentleman is working in the greenhouse, sir. I thought he was joking the other day when he asked if he could put up a vice on the potting bench, but, lord, he's been busy ever since!"

"He's inventing a new carburettor," said Manfred, devoutly hoping that the lady had no knowledge of the internal-combustion engine.

"He's working hard, too, sir; he came out to get a breath of air just now, and I never saw a gentleman perspire so! He seems to be working with that file all the day."

"You mustn't interrupt him," began Manfred.

"I shouldn't dream of doing it," said the landlady indignantly.

Manfred made his way to the garden, and his friend, who saw him coming – the greenhouse made an ideal workshop for Leon, for he could watch his landlady's approach and conceal the key he had been filing for three days – walked to meet him.

"He is leaving today, or rather tonight," said Manfred. "He's going to Plymouth: there he will catch the Holland-American boat to New York."

"Tonight?" said Leon in surprise. "That cuts me rather fine. By what train?"

"That I don't know," said Manfred.

"You're sure?"

Manfred nodded.

"He's giving it out that he's leaving tomorrow, and is slipping away tonight. I don't think he wants people to know of his departure. I discovered it through an indiscretion of the worthy doctor's. I was in the post office when he was sending a wire. He had his pocket-book open on the counter, and I saw some labels peeping out. I knew they were steamship labels, and I glimpsed the printed word 'Rotterdam', looked up the newspapers, and saw that the *Rotterdam* was leaving tomorrow. When I heard that he had told people that he was leaving Newton Abbot tomorrow I was certain."

"That's all to the good," said Leon. "George, we're going to achieve the crowning deed of our lives. I say 'we', but I'm afraid I must do this alone – though you have a very important rôle to play."

He chuckled softly and rubbed his hands.

"Like every other clever criminal he has made one of the most stupid of blunders. He has inherited his wife's money under an old will, which left him all her possessions, with the exception of £2,000 which she had on deposit at the bank, and this went to her nephew, the Plymouth engineer. In his greed Twenden is pretty certain to have forgotten this legacy. He's got all the money in a Torquay bank. It was transferred from Newton Abbot a few days ago and was the talk of the town. Go to Plymouth, interview young Jacley, see his lawyer, if he has one, or any lawyer if he hasn't, and if the two thousand pounds has not been paid, get him to apply for a warrant for Twenden's arrest. He is an absconding trustee under those circumstances, and the Justices will grant the warrant if they know the man is leaving by the *Rotterdam* tomorrow."

"If you were an ordinary man, Leon," said Manfred, "I should think that your revenge was a little inadequate."

"It will not be that," said Leon quietly.

At nine-thirty, Dr Twenden, with his coat collar turned up and the brim of a felt hat hiding the upper part of his face, was entering a first-class carriage at Newton Abbot, when the local detective-sergeant whom he knew tapped him on the shoulder.

"I want you, Doctor."

"Why, Sergeant?" demanded the doctor, suddenly white.

"I have a warrant for your arrest," said the officer.

When the charge was read over to the man at the police station he raved like a lunatic.

"I'll give you the money now, now! I must go tonight. I'm leaving for America tomorrow."

"So I gather," said the Inspector dryly. "That is why you're arrested, Doctor."

And they locked him in the cells for the night.

The next morning he was brought before the Justices. Evidence was taken, the young nephew from Plymouth made his statement, and the Justices conferred.

"There is prima facie evidence here of intention to defraud, Dr Twenden," said the chairman at last. "You are arrested with a very large sum of money and letters of credit in your possession, and it seems clear that it was your intention to leave the country. Under those circumstances we have no other course to follow, but commit you to take your trial at the forthcoming session."

"But I can have bail: I insist upon that," said the doctor furiously.

"There will be no bail," was the sharp reply, and that afternoon he was removed by taxicab to Baxeter prison.

The Sessions were for the following week, and the doctor again fumed in that very prison from which he had emerged if not with credit, at least without disaster.

On the second day of his incarceration the Governor of Baxeter Gaol received a message:

"Six star men transferred to you will arrive at Baxeter Station 10.15. Arrange for prison van to meet."

It was signed "Imprison", which is the telegraphic address of the Prison Commissioner.

It happened that just about then there had been a mutiny in one of the London prisons, and the deputy governor, beyond expressing his surprise as to the lateness of the hour, arranged for the prison van to be at Baxeter station yard to meet the batch of transfers.

The 10.15 from London drew into the station, and the warders waiting on the platform walked slowly down the train looking for a carriage with drawn blinds. But there were no prisoners on the train, and there was no other train due until four o'clock in the morning.

"They must have missed it," said one of the warders. "All right, Jerry," this to the driver. He slammed the door of the Black Maria which had been left open, and the van lumbered out of the station yard.

Slowly up the slope and through the black prison gates: the van turned through another gate to the left, a gate set at right angles to the first, and stopped before the open doors of a brick shed isolated from the prison.

The driver grumbled as he descended and unharnessed his horses.

"I shan't put the van in the shed tonight," he said. "Perhaps you'll get some of the prisoners to do it tomorrow."

"That will be all right," said the warder, anxious to get away.

The horses went clopping from the place of servitude, there was a snap of locks as the gates were closed, and then silence.

So far all was well from one man's point of view. A roaring south-wester was blowing down from Dartmoor round the angles of the prison, and wailing through the dark, deserted yard.

Suddenly there was a gentle crack, and the door of the Black Maria opened. Leon had discovered that his key could not open yet another door. He had slipped into the prison van when the warders were searching the train, and had found some difficulty in getting out again. No men were coming from London, as he knew, but he was desperately in need of that Black Maria. It had piloted him to the very spot he wished to go. He listened. There was no sound save the wind, and he walked cautiously to a little glass-covered building, and plied his master key. The lock turned, and he was inside a small recess where the prisoners were photographed. Through another door, and he was in a storeroom. Beyond that lay the prison wards. He had questioned wisely and knew where the remand cells were to be found.

A patrol would pass soon, he thought, looking at his watch, and waited till he heard footsteps go by the door. The patrol would now be traversing a wing at right angles to the ward, and he opened the door and stepped into the deserted hall. He heard the feet of the patrol man receding and went softly up a flight of iron stairs to the floor above and along the cell doors. Presently he saw the man he wanted. His key went noiselessly into the cell door and turned. Doctor Twenden blinked up at him from his wooden bed.

"Get up," whispered Gonsalez, "and turn round."

Numbly the doctor obeyed.

Leon strapped his hands behind him and took him by the arm, stopping to lock the cell door. Out through the storeroom into the little glass place, then before the doctor knew what had happened, he slipped a large silk handkerchief over his mouth.

"Can you hear me?"

The man nodded.

"Can you feel that?"

"That" was something sharp that stabbed his left arm. He tried to wriggle his arm away.

"You will recognise the value of a hypodermic syringe, you better than any," said the voice of Gonsalez in his ear. "You murdered an innocent woman, and you evaded the law. A few days ago you spoke of the Four Just Men. I am one of them!"

The man stared into the darkness at a face he could not see.

"The law missed you, but we have not missed you. Can you understand?"

The head nodded more slowly now.

Leon released his grip of the man's arm, and felt him slipping to the floor. There he lay whilst Gonsalez went into the shed, pulled up the two traps that hung straightly in the pit until they clicked together, and slipped the end of the rope he had worn round his waist over the beam…

Then he went back to the unconscious man.

In the morning when the warders came to the coach-house, which was also the execution shed, they saw a taut rope. The trap was open, and a man was at the end of the rope, very still. A man who had escaped the gallows of the law, but had died at the hands of justice.

Edgar Wallace

Big Foot

Footprints and a dead woman bring together Superintendent Minton and the amateur sleuth Mr Cardew. Who is the man in the shrubbery? Who is the singer of the haunting Moorish tune? Why is Hannah Shaw so determined to go to Pawsy, 'a dog lonely place' she had previously detested? Death lurks in the dark and someone must solve the mystery before BIG FOOT strikes again, in a yet more fiendish manner.

Bones In London

The new Managing Director of Schemes Ltd has an elegant London office and a theatrically dressed assistant – however, Bones, as he is better known, is bored. Luckily there is a slump in the shipping market and it is not long before Joe and Fred Pole pay Bones a visit. They are totally unprepared for Bones' unnerving style of doing business, unprepared for his unique style of innocent and endearing mischief.

EDGAR WALLACE

BONES OF THE RIVER

'Taking the little paper from the pigeon's leg, Hamilton saw it was from Sanders and marked URGENT. *Send Bones instantly to Lujamalababa… Arrest and bring to headquarters the witch doctor.*'

It is a time when the world's most powerful nations are vying for colonial honour, a time of trading steamers and tribal chiefs. In the mysterious African territories administered by Commissioner Sanders, Bones persistently manages to create his own unique style of innocent and endearing mischief.

THE DAFFODIL MYSTERY

When Mr Thomas Lyne, poet, poseur and owner of Lyne's Emporium insults a cashier, Odette Rider, she resigns. Having summoned detective Jack Tarling to investigate another employee, Mr Milburgh, Lyne now changes his plans. Tarling and his Chinese companion refuse to become involved. They pay a visit to Odette's flat and in the hall Tarling meets Sam, convicted felon and protégé of Lyne. Next morning Tarling discovers a body. The hands are crossed on the breast, adorned with a handful of daffodils.

Edgar Wallace

The Joker
(USA: The Colossus)

While the millionaire Stratford Harlow is in Princetown, not only does he meet with his lawyer Mr Ellenbury but he gets his first glimpse of the beautiful Aileen Rivers, niece of the actor and convicted felon Arthur Ingle. When Aileen is involved in a car accident on the Thames Embankment, the driver is James Carlton of Scotland Yard. Later that evening Carlton gets a call. It is Aileen. She needs help.

The Square Emerald
(USA: The Girl From Scotland Yard)

'Suicide on the left,' says Chief Inspector Coldwell pleasantly, as he and Leslie Maughan stride along the Thames Embankment during a brutally cold night. A gaunt figure is sprawled across the parapet. But Coldwell soon discovers that Peter Dawlish, fresh out of prison for forgery, is not considering suicide but murder. Coldwell suspects Druze as the intended victim. Maughan disagrees. If Druze dies, she says, 'It will be because he does not love children!'

OTHER TITLES BY EDGAR WALLACE AVAILABLE DIRECT
FROM HOUSE OF STRATUS

Quantity		£	$(US)	$(CAN)	€
	THE ADMIRABLE CARFEW	6.99	12.95	19.95	13.50
	THE ANGEL OF TERROR	6.99	12.95	19.95	13.50
	THE AVENGER *(USA: THE HAIRY ARM)*	6.99	12.95	19.95	13.50
	BARBARA ON HER OWN	6.99	12.95	19.95	13.50
	BIG FOOT	6.99	12.95	19.95	13.50
	THE BLACK ABBOT	6.99	12.95	19.95	13.50
	BONES	6.99	12.95	19.95	13.50
	BONES IN LONDON	6.99	12.95	19.95	13.50
	BONES OF THE RIVER	6.99	12.95	19.95	13.50
	THE CLUE OF THE NEW PIN	6.99	12.95	19.95	13.50
	THE CLUE OF THE SILVER KEY	6.99	12.95	19.95	13.50
	THE CLUE OF THE TWISTED CANDLE	6.99	12.95	19.95	13.50
	THE COAT OF ARMS				
	(USA: THE ARRANWAYS MYSTERY)	6.99	12.95	19.95	13.50
	THE COUNCIL OF JUSTICE	6.99	12.95	19.95	13.50
	THE CRIMSON CIRCLE	6.99	12.95	19.95	13.50
	THE DAFFODIL MYSTERY	6.99	12.95	19.95	13.50
	THE DARK EYES OF LONDON				
	(USA: THE CROAKERS)	6.99	12.95	19.95	13.50
	THE DAUGHTERS OF THE NIGHT	6.99	12.95	19.95	13.50
	A DEBT DISCHARGED	6.99	12.95	19.95	13.50
	THE DEVIL MAN	6.99	12.95	19.95	13.50
	THE DOOR WITH SEVEN LOCKS	6.99	12.95	19.95	13.50
	THE DUKE IN THE SUBURBS	6.99	12.95	19.95	13.50
	THE FACE IN THE NIGHT	6.99	12.95	19.95	13.50
	THE FEATHERED SERPENT	6.99	12.95	19.95	13.50
	THE FLYING SQUAD	6.99	12.95	19.95	13.50
	THE FORGER *(USA: THE CLEVER ONE)*	6.99	12.95	19.95	13.50
	THE FOUR JUST MEN	6.99	12.95	19.95	13.50
	FOUR SQUARE JANE	6.99	12.95	19.95	13.50

ALL HOUSE OF STRATUS BOOKS ARE AVAILABLE FROM GOOD BOOKSHOPS
OR DIRECT FROM THE PUBLISHER:

Internet: www.houseofstratus.com including synopses and features.

Email: sales@houseofstratus.com
info@houseofstratus.com
(please quote author, title and credit card details.)

OTHER TITLES BY EDGAR WALLACE AVAILABLE DIRECT
FROM HOUSE OF STRATUS

Quantity		£	$(US)	$(CAN)	€
	THE FOURTH PLAGUE	6.99	12.95	19.95	13.50
	THE FRIGHTENED LADY	6.99	12.95	19.95	13.50
	GOOD EVANS	6.99	12.95	19.95	13.50
	THE HAND OF POWER	6.99	12.95	19.95	13.50
	THE IRON GRIP	6.99	12.95	19.95	13.50
	THE JOKER (USA: THE COLOSSUS)	6.99	12.95	19.95	13.50
	THE JUST MEN OF CORDOVA	6.99	12.95	19.95	13.50
	THE KEEPERS OF THE KING'S PEACE	6.99	12.95	19.95	13.50
	THE LONE HOUSE MYSTERY	6.99	12.95	19.95	13.50
	THE MAN WHO BOUGHT LONDON	6.99	12.95	19.95	13.50
	THE MAN WHO KNEW	6.99	12.95	19.95	13.50
	THE MAN WHO WAS NOBODY	6.99	12.95	19.95	13.50
	THE MIND OF MR J G REEDER				
	(USA: THE MURDER BOOK OF J G REEDER)	6.99	12.95	19.95	13.50
	MORE EDUCATED EVANS	6.99	12.95	19.95	13.50
	MR J G REEDER RETURNS				
	(USA: MR REEDER RETURNS)	6.99	12.95	19.95	13.50
	MR JUSTICE MAXELL	6.99	12.95	19.95	13.50
	RED ACES	6.99	12.95	19.95	13.50
	ROOM 13	6.99	12.95	19.95	13.50
	SANDERS	6.99	12.95	19.95	13.50
	SANDERS OF THE RIVER	6.99	12.95	19.95	13.50
	THE SINISTER MAN	6.99	12.95	19.95	13.50
	THE SQUARE EMERALD				
	(USA: THE GIRL FROM SCOTLAND YARD)	6.99	12.95	19.95	13.50
	THE THREE JUST MEN	6.99	12.95	19.95	13.50
	THE THREE OAK MYSTERY	6.99	12.95	19.95	13.50
	THE TRAITOR'S GATE	6.99	12.95	19.95	13.50
	WHEN THE GANGS CAME TO LONDON	6.99	12.95	19.95	13.50

Tel: Order Line
            0800 169 1780 (UK)
             800 724 1100 (USA)
            International
            +44 (0) 1845 527700 (UK)
            +01   845 463 1100 (USA)

Fax: +44 (0) 1845 527711 (UK)
            +01   845 463 0018 (USA)
            (please quote author, title and credit card details.)

Send to: House of Stratus Sales Department
            Thirsk Industrial Park
            York Road, Thirsk
            North Yorkshire, YO7 3BX
            UK

PAYMENT

Please tick currency you wish to use:

☐ £ (Sterling)   ☐ $ (US)   ☐ $ (CAN)   ☐ € (Euros)

Allow for shipping costs charged per order plus an amount per book as set out in the tables below:

CURRENCY/DESTINATION

	£(Sterling)	$(US)	$(CAN)	€ (Euros)
Cost per order				
UK	1.50	2.25	3.50	2.50
Europe	3.00	4.50	6.75	5.00
North America	3.00	3.50	5.25	5.00
Rest of World	3.00	4.50	6.75	5.00
Additional cost per book				
UK	0.50	0.75	1.15	0.85
Europe	1.00	1.50	2.25	1.70
North America	1.00	1.00	1.50	1.70
Rest of World	1.50	2.25	3.50	3.00

PLEASE SEND CHEQUE OR INTERNATIONAL MONEY ORDER
payable to: HOUSE OF STRATUS LTD or HOUSE OF STRATUS INC. or card payment as indicated

STERLING EXAMPLE

Cost of book(s):..................... Example: 3 x books at £6.99 each: £20.97
Cost of order: .... Example: £1.50 (Delivery to UK address)
Additional cost per book:.............. Example: 3 x £0.50; £1.50
Order total including shipping:.......... Example: £23.97

VISA, MASTERCARD, SWITCH, AMEX:

☐☐☐☐☐☐☐☐☐☐☐☐☐☐☐☐☐☐☐

Issue number (Switch only):

☐☐☐

Start Date: Expiry Date:

☐☐/☐☐   ☐☐/☐☐

Signature: _____

NAME: _____

ADDRESS: _____

COUNTRY: _____

ZIP/POSTCODE: _____

Please allow 28 days for delivery. Despatch normally within 48 hours.

Prices subject to change without notice.
Please tick box if you do not wish to receive any additional information. ☐

House of Stratus publishes many other titles in this genre; please check our website (**www.houseofstratus.com**) for more details.